Holly

A NOVELLA

SEASONS OF LOVE
BOOK ONE

C.L. COLLIER

This book is a work of fiction. Names, characters, places, and incidents are products of the author's imagination and are used fictitiously. Any resemblance to actual events or locales or persons, living or dead, is entirely coincidental and beyond the intent of the author or publisher.

Editing by Jenny Sims, Editing 4 Indies

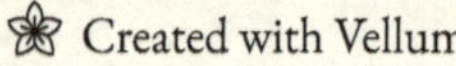

I dedicate this book to my sister, Nina.
Thanks for putting up with me, always being supportive, and all the fun times we had growing up and continue to have as adults! I'm lucky to have you in my life!

About Holly

Holly was previously included in *XOXO*, a multi-author limited edition anthology, which is longer available to purchase.

Holly

I never expected to move back to my hometown, but things have a funny way of working out sometimes.

I also never expected to run into Patrick Dye--Port Townsend's own football star turned pro-football player.

And I definitely never thought he'd recognize me after all these years, or that he'd ask me out.

In this season of unexpected changes, I might have met my perfect match with Patrick.

With every season comes love--eventually. Find out how sisters Holly, Summer, Autumn, and April each find love when they least expect it in the Seasons of Love Series by C.L. Collier.

Holly

Welcome home. As I drive off the ferry toward Water Street, it feels different. Unlike all the times I came home to visit over the past six years, I'm staying this time. My car is packed full of my belongings, and I'm back in my hometown indefinitely. It's time to figure out what I really want to do with my life.

This past year has been a difficult one. After graduating from college with my Bachelor's in Education degree, I accepted my first teaching job. I was ecstatic, to say the least, to be offered a job straight out of college. The school I student taught at added another fourth-grade position. It was like a dream come true to get a job right away, especially at the school I had come to love working at.

However, things didn't work as well as I had hoped. Nothing was quite the same as it had been for me as a student teacher. Some of the students in my class had more discipline issues than I was prepared to deal with, and the stress grew on me. Although I had support from my colleagues, admin, and the school's instructional coach, I realized that teaching wasn't turning out to be exactly what I had signed up for. By spring, I was at my wit's end. After talking with a couple of friends and my sisters, I decided it would be a good idea to resign at the end of the school year, then take some time to think about what I want to do with my life.

I was living in Seattle with one of my sisters, April, but it was our other sister, Summer, who talked me into moving back home to Port Townsend. After careful consideration, I decided to take Summer's advice, as well as accept her offer of moving in with her. I don't know where I'd be without my sisters--all three of them. Summer is the only one who's living in Port Townsend, though. April is two years older than me and lives in Seattle, and Autumn, the oldest of us four girls, is the farthest away in Portland. No matter how close or far we all are in distance from one another, though, we still stay in close contact.

As I drive up the hill toward Summer's house, I'm suddenly hit with a feeling of homesickness. It's a strange feeling since I'm back in the town where I was born and raised. However, I've called Seattle home my whole adult life so far, and moving back to Port Townsend gives me mixed emotions. After all, I thought I was destined to be Holly Seasons, Super Teacher. I didn't expect to move back home, jobless and not sure what to do with my life.

I pull up to the old Victorian house Summer has been renting for the past couple of years and park in front, along the curb. I guess it was my luck that her best friend and former roommate got married last month and moved out, leaving room for me to move in. It worked out so perfectly, it felt as if it was meant for me to move back here.

After grabbing my purse and the small box of makeup

and toiletries from the passenger seat, I walk up to the front porch. Before I set foot on the first stair, the front door swings open, and Summer walks out. "You're here!" She greets me with a warm smile.

I climb the steps and meet her on the porch. "I'm here. Are you ready for me?"

Summer wraps me in a hug. "Of course I am. I'm excited to have you as my new roomie." Dropping her arms, she asks, "Can I help you carry stuff in?"

"My car's full," I say with a short laugh. "Grab whatever you can carry."

"I'll show you to your room first," she says, then leads me into the house.

I've been to Summer's apartment before, which takes up the entire main floor of this old Victorian home. The upstairs is another rental and so is the basement, each with its own separate entrance. Summer's apartment consists of a living room, kitchen, dining room, two bedrooms, and a bathroom. I always thought its historic charm was adorable, and I'm excited to live here with her.

Summer leads me down the short hallway to my bedroom. "Here you go," she says as we walk into the room. "Hopefully, the bed is comfortable for you. It was nice of Jessie to sell her furniture to you."

"I'm sure it'll be fine," I reply, setting my box and purse on the mattress. Since Jessie got married and she and her husband bought a new bedroom set, she left her full-size bed, nightstand, and dresser here for me. That way, I didn't have to move my furniture from Seattle, making it easier to move without having to haul any furniture. I sold my bedroom set in Seattle, then sent the money to Jessie to buy her set from her. It couldn't have worked out more perfectly.

"Let's go unload your car," Summer says, and we both head back outside to start moving my things in.

* * *

"I'm so glad to have you back here," Summer says as she drives downtown for dinner.

"It's good to be back," I reply. "Now I just need to find a job."

"At least you have some time to do that. You're still getting paid through August?"

I nod. "Yeah. I'd like to find a job soon, though. Otherwise, I know I'll get bored, then it'll be harder to get back into the workforce. I haven't had a summer off since I was in middle school." I chuckle at the realization.

"What do you think you'd like to do?" she asks.

"Honestly, I'm open to anything. I just want to take a break from teaching so I can consider other professions."

"I wish we were hiring at the library," Summer says as she pulls into a parking lot. "Although, even if we were, you'd probably need a degree in library science in order to be considered."

"That's okay. I'll find something."

Summer parks her car. She's been a librarian at the public library in town for about six years now. After she graduated from college with her library science degree, she moved back home and was lucky to get hired right away. I considered majoring in library science after I saw how much she enjoyed it, but I decided to go with my first choice of education. Now, I wish I had chosen a different path.

We make our way to the entrance of The Cellar, one of the more popular restaurants and bars in town. It's one of my favorite places to eat, and I get a little excited when I notice the "now hiring" sign on the door.

"Oh, look at that," Summer says, pointing at the sign. "You have serving experience."

"I'll ask them about it," I say as we walk in. I worked as a server all through college, and before that, I was a restaurant hostess in high school. I really enjoyed the job--and the tips--and it's a job I've considered doing again. Hopefully, that's what they're hiring for.

We seat ourselves, as the sign up front instructs us to do, and find a booth to sit at in the back of the restaurant. As usual, the place is busy, but at least we don't have to wait for a table. As soon as the server brings us menus, I ask her about the open position.

"We're hiring for a server," she says. "Why? Are you interested?"

I smile at her. "Yes, I am. I just moved back to town, and I need a job."

"Awesome. I'll let the owner, Shawna, know. She's still here in the back."

"Shawna Sparks?" I ask, realizing I think I know the owner from high school.

"Yeah, do you know her?"

Oh, thank goodness. I remember Shawna's dad owned this place, so she must be a co-owner now. This could help my chances of getting the job. "I do. I'm not sure if she'll remember me since I was a year behind her, but we went to high school together."

"Cool. What's your name? I'll go tell Shawna now before she leaves."

"Holly Seasons. She may not remember me, though."

"I'll go talk to her now." Our server smiles kindly, then turns and walks away.

Summer looks at me, wide eyed. "Wow. This may work out really well for you!"

I shrug, trying not to get my hopes up ... although I have a giddy feeling that this may be my lucky day.

"Living in a small town has its advantages," Summer says, then looks down at her menu.

I look at my menu as well, but before I've decided whether I want to order the salmon or the French dip, I hear my name.

"Holly Seasons!" I look up to see Shawna Sparks approaching our table. She looks the same as I remember, just a little older. "How are you? I hear you're looking for a job!"

"I'm good! I just moved back to town--today, actually--and I need to find a job."

"Wow. Welcome back to Port Townsend. Do you have any experience working as a server?"

"I do," I tell her, then go on to explain that I worked as a server in Seattle all five years of college.

"That's awesome. So you went to school in Seattle?" she asks.

"Yeah, I graduated from PNWU. I got my degree in education, but after teaching this past school year, I realized it wasn't exactly what I expected it to be. I decided to come home and take a break from it while I figure out what else to do with my life."

"So back to serving?" Shawna says with a laugh.

I can't help but laugh as well. "Yeah, I guess so. But don't get me wrong--I enjoyed working as a server, and I'd love the opportunity to do it again."

Shawna looks as though she's considering what I said. Then she looks at Summer. "Oh, sorry. I forgot my manners." She puts her hand out for Summer to shake. "I'm Shawna."

Summer shakes her hand. "It's nice to meet you. I'm Holly's sister Summer."

Shawna's eyes get big and she looks as though she just remembered something. "That's right! You're the Seasons sisters!"

Summer and I both chuckle. That's what the four of us were known as growing up, not only because it's our last name, but because our parents were somewhat clever with what they named each of us.

"How could I forget?" Shawna says, shaking her head. She points at Summer. "I think you graduated before I was in high school, but your other sister, April, was a year ahead of me, right?" She looks at me, squinting her eyes as if she's trying to remember.

"Yes, that's right," I explain. "I'm the youngest. April is two years older than me, which makes her one year older than you. Summer is three years older than April, and our oldest sister, Autumn--"

"Is two years older than me," Summer says, completing my sentence.

Shawna smiles. "Do all of you still live here in town?"

Summer and I both shake our heads, then she answers, "No. April lives in Seattle, and Autumn is down in Portland."

Shawna nods. "I always thought your names were so cool. Your parents were sure--"

"Crazy?" I interject with a laugh, and Summer and Shawna laugh too.

"No, no," Shawna says, shaking her head. "I was going to say creative."

"Yeah, well being named Summer Seasons came with its fair share of jokes growing up," Summer says. "But it's definitely original."

"I suppose so," Shawna replies. "How did they come up with your names, anyway?"

"Well, Autumn was born in October," I explain. "Because of our last name, Mom thought it would be fun to name her after the season she was born in."

"Then I was born in June," Summer continues. "So the season name worked again. When April came along, they considered naming her Spring since she was born in April, but Mom liked the name April better."

"Her middle name is Spring, though," I add with a chuckle.

Shawna looks at me. "How did they come up with your name?"

"I was born in December, and thankfully, Mom and Dad decided *not* to name me that. They considered several names having to do with the holiday season and settled on Holly Noelle."

"That's a pretty name. You *all* have pretty and unique names. I think that's really awesome," Shawna says.

"Thanks," Summer and I say in unison.

"Well, anyway," Shawna says with a quick shake of her head. Then she looks at me again. "About the job. Are you available to come by tomorrow morning at around ten?"

"Sure! That works for me," I say, hopeful that she's offering me the job.

"Great! Come in then, and I'll show you around. I think this may work out really

well to add you to The Cellar's staff."

My smile widens. "Thank you so much! I'll be here at ten."

"Great! See you tomorrow, Holly." She says goodbye to Summer, then turns and walks away.

"Wow, you got a job already!" Summer's eyes widen in astonishment.

"I guess so," I say. "As long as everything goes well tomorrow, I suppose I do."

Hopefully, this is a sign of good things to come.

Holly

Six months later...

"Happy New Year!"

I never liked working on New Year's Eve when I was in college, but working at The Cellar is more fun than I thought it would be. Not only is it karaoke night but everyone who showed up to bring in the new year has been fun and great to wait on. It's felt more like a party than a work shift.

These past six months have been nothing but great for me. I love my job, I love living with Summer, and I love being back in Port Townsend. Although none of my friends from high school live here anymore, I've made new friends. Shawna and I have become somewhat close. Our lives are very different, though, since she has a fiancé and young son at home, so we don't hang out outside of work. Another server I work with, Kayla, and I have hung out a few times, and I consider her a friend. We're the same age, although she didn't grow up in Port Townsend. She moved here from Chimacum, a nearby town so small that it makes Port Townsend seem like a big city.

Although I love my job, I often wonder if I made the right choice to quit teaching. A part of me wonders if I should give it another try. After all, maybe it will be different in Port Townsend than in Seattle. However, I don't know if I should sign up as a substitute teacher. I enjoy my days off, and I'm not sure I'm ready to give teaching another try yet.

"Hey, can we get two more margaritas, please?" one of the customers I've been waiting on all night asks as I walk toward the bar to input another order.

"You got it," I say with a smile.

After I give my orders to the bartender, I turn around and look at the sea of people watching the lady on stage singing "Quit Playing Games" by the Backstreet Boys. She sounds horrible, but she's having fun, and the crowd is being kind to her. Now that it's after midnight, most people here are drunk and singing along.

As I wait for the drinks to be made, I look around at everyone. Most people are standing, watching the karaoke stage, but a few are sitting at the bar. One man sitting opposite me looks familiar, and it doesn't take long for me to realize who he is.

Patrick Dye.

He graduated from high school a year before me. He was a star football player and even played professionally with the Rainier Renegades for a while before he was injured. I didn't know he moved back to Port Townsend ... or maybe he's just visiting. He's still as handsome as he was back in high school. All the girls--including myself--had crushes on him back then. He never gave me the time of day, though. We had a few classes together over the years, but I doubt he'd recognize me now as easily as I recognized him.

He takes a drink of his beer, and as he sets the glass in front of him, his eyes look up and meet mine. My stomach flip flops as Patrick does a double take. I wonder if he actually knows who I am.

"Here you go," Jalen, the bartender, says, blocking my view of Patrick as he sets two drinks on my tray.

I'm quickly brought back to reality. "Thanks. I'm waiting for two margaritas, too," I remind Jalen.

"Comin' up," he says, saluting me before turning around to make the drinks.

My view of Patrick is clear, but unfortunately, he's not there anymore. He must've left. It's just as well. I'm not sure what could've possibly happened between us anyway.

"Hey, I know you," a deep voice cuts through the karaoke singing, and I look to my right to see who it is.

My mouth goes dry as Patrick Dye is standing mere inches from me.

"You grew up here, didn't you?" he asks, and I realize he's talking to me.

My hand flies to my chest. "Me?" I look around to make sure I'm not standing next to someone else he would know.

"Yeah, you," he says, reminding me of Jake Ryan in *Sixteen Candles.* My sisters and I watched that movie countless times growing up. We found our mom's DVD copy and after watching it once we were obsessed.

Still surprised that he's speaking to me, I reply, "Um... yeah, I did. Are you Patrick Dye?" I know it's him, but I have to ask so he doesn't think I'm a crazy stalker or something.

His smile widens. "Yeah, I am. So you remember me, too?"

I nod, swallowing hard, trying not to let on that I'm nervous as hell to have *the* Patrick Dye, *football star*, striking up a conversation with me. "You were a year ahead of me."

"I thought so," he replies. "You're one of the Seasons sisters, right?"

I'm seriously shocked he knows who I am. "That's right," I say before Jalen steals my attention by setting two more drinks on my tray.

"There you go, Holly," he says with a wink before turning around again.

Remembering I have a job to do that doesn't involve getting lost in Patrick Dye's sexy good looks, I pick my tray up, balancing it in my left hand. "Sorry, I have to go deliver these," I tell Patrick as I start to walk away.

As I pass by him, he says, "I'll be here."

He's going to wait for me to come back?

I walk through the crowd of people to deliver the drinks to my customers, all the while in a daze. How does Patrick remember me? We barely spoke to each other growing up. Is he just shooting his shot, hoping to hook up with someone tonight? I hope not. He remembered my last name, as well as the nickname for my sisters and me. Maybe he genuinely remembers who I am.

Once my tray is empty, I walk back toward the bar. The lady finishes "Quit Playing Games," and everyone cheers for her. I tuck my tray under my arm and clap as well. Anyone who has the nerve to sing in front of a crowd deserves praise. I, for one, have never sung karaoke because I know how horrible I'd sound. Singing was never my forte.

As I walk back toward the bar, I wonder if Patrick is, in fact, still there waiting for me. If he is, I should continue talking with him. I don't want to be rude, and I'm curious to find out how much he remembers about me.

I see him sitting on a barstool exactly where I left him moments ago. He's looking in my direction, and once he makes eye contact, he smiles. Gathering all the confidence I can muster, I walk directly over to him and set my tray on the bar.

"So what is Patrick Dye doing here in The Cellar on New Year's Eve?" I ask, placing my hand on my hip. "Are you just visiting, or did you move back to town?"

Patrick's eyebrows shoot upward. "Wow, you knew that I moved away?"

He's got to be kidding. *Everyone* in Port Townsend knew he moved away to play football. I'm pretty sure there was a parade in his honor before he left for college.

With a roll of my eyes, I reply, "Yes, just like the rest of the town was aware that Patrick Dye left to pursue his football career. You're kind of famous, you know."

He smirks. "I suppose you're right. I don't know about being famous, though." He pauses to take a sip of his beer. "But to answer your question, I moved back to town a couple of years ago."

I nod, wondering what he's been doing since his football career ended. The crowd erupts in cheers as "Pour Some Sugar on Me" blasts over the sound system. I turn around and see a middle-aged guy on stage with short hair and glasses wearing a button-up shirt. He reminds me of Bill Gates, not someone about to belt out a Def Lepard classic. However, as he starts singing, it's clear he's done this before––and he's good.

Patrick and I watch as he entertains the crowd. He's captivating the audience, probably because no one expected him to put on such a good performance. Everyone begins singing along, including Patrick and me. It occurs to me that I'm still on the clock, but no one seems to need anything, so I enjoy the moment along with everyone else.

As Bill Gates finishes the song, lunging with his free hand raised in the air like a true rock star, the crowd goes wild. Everyone settles down when he walks off the stage, and I turn around toward Patrick again.

"That was incredible," he says. "I didn't expect such a performance from that guy."

"Neither did I," I say with a laugh. "So ... are you going to give it a try? Sing a little song?"

Patrick shakes his head. "No way. I'm not a singer. How about you?"

I shake my head as well. "Nope. Same for me ... I don't sing."

"Well, what *are* you good at?" he asks with a playful grin. "You know I played football. What about you?"

I put my finger to my chin as I consider how to answer his question. "Well," I say, putting my finger down, "I didn't play any sports growing up, but I *did* take dance lessons all the way through high school."

"You did? That's pretty cool," Patrick says. "What kind of dance?"

"Ballet, mostly. But I did a little bit of tap for a while, too."

"That's awesome. Do you still do any dancing?"

The way he asks me sounds as if he's insinuating something. "What do you

mean?" I ask, putting a hand on my hip.

Patrick looks confused. "Like ... do you still dance?" he asks, shrugging one shoulder.

Maybe he didn't mean anything by it.

"No, I don't. I haven't since high school."

Just then, a customer waves at me.

"Sorry, I need to go take care of a customer," I tell Patrick.

"It's okay. Maybe I'll see you around," he says, giving me a subtle chin nod.

As I walk away, I wonder if I will see him again. That was bizarre. I can't believe I had a conversation with Patrick Dye, and he knew who I was.

Patrick sticks around while I finish the rest of my shift. He's friendly with Jalen, as well as some of the other customers. He seems like a genuinely nice guy, but I wonder why he chooses to stick around so late, especially after everyone else leaves and just us employees are here to close the place down. In fact, he offers to help clean up. Why is he doing this? I don't complain, though. With Patrick's help, we're able to leave much sooner than I thought we would.

I'm not used to working so late, and I'm exhausted. It's nearly three o'clock, and all I want to do is crawl into my comfy bed and go to sleep. As we all walk out to the parking lot, everyone says goodbye to each other and then heads to their cars. As I walk to mine, I notice Patrick walking away to where no cars are parked. Curious as to where he's going, I call out, "Hey, Patrick! Do you need a ride?" After all, it's three in the morning. No one should have to walk home.

He stops and turns back toward me. "No, I'm good!"

What the hell?

He turns around and starts walking again, but I can't stand it. "Seriously?" I call out, and he stops again.

Patrick turns around, and to my surprise, he starts to jog toward me. The smug look on his face conflicts me. I'm not sure what to think of Patrick Dye after tonight, but one thing's for sure--I'm still just as attracted to him now as I was in high school.

My coworkers all begin to drive away. As Patrick approaches me, I realize we're the only two people left in the parking lot.

"Are you concerned about me getting home safely?" he asks with a playful smirk on his face.

Damn him for giving me butterflies.

"Well, how far away do you live? No one should have to walk home this late at night."

He chuckles once, but then his eyes catch something behind me and his face looks more serious. "Oh, shit," he says, causing me to turn and look at what he saw.

Fuck. My stomach drops as I see the deflated tire on my car.

"Looks like you have a flat," he says, stating the obvious.

"Shit." I march the short distance to my car, all the while trying to remember the steps in changing a tire. My dad taught me when I was sixteen, but I've yet to have to do it on my own. Not only was that almost a decade ago but I'm also exhausted. My brain is mush.

"Do you need a hand?" Patrick asks, walking up behind me.

Rubbing my forehead, I'm not even sure if I know how

to get my spare out of the trunk. "Yeah, that'd be great," I say, grateful he's here to help.

"Pop your trunk," he says, so I do.

Patrick gets right to work, seeming to know exactly what to do.

"Your trunk is clean," he comments.

"Yeah, I'm a bit of a neat freak," I say with a laugh before a yawn escapes.

Patrick glances at me as he pulls my spare tire out of the trunk. "Am I boring you?" he asks, setting the tire on the ground before walking back to my trunk to retrieve something else.

Shaking my head, I reply. "No, of course not. I'm just exhausted. Honestly, I'm relieved you're here to help me."

Patrick appears again, holding the car jack in one hand and the tool that I know loosens the lug nuts--or whatever those things are called--in the other. God, I feel like a complete idiot. I need to have Dad re-teach me how to change a tire. I should be able to do this on my own without depending on anyone else to help me. What if this happened when I was all alone? I'd be screwed right now. Who knows how long it would take for someone to come help me at this time of night.

"I'm glad I'm here to help you," Patrick says as he kneels and gets to work.

I pay attention to what he's doing, hoping I can re-learn the steps of changing a tire by watching him. Neither of us says anything as I watch, and he concentrates on what he's doing. Once he removes the lug nuts, he asks me to hold them.

As he puts the spare tire on, I remember my wondering

from earlier before we discovered my flat tire. "So were you going to walk all the way home?" I ask him.

He cracks a smile, but doesn't look at me as he continues to work. "Yeah, I was. And I will after I finish getting this tire on for you."

Confused as to why he'd still refuse a ride home, I ask, "Why? The least I can do after all your help is drive you home."

Patrick doesn't say anything as he tightens the last lug nut. Once he's done, he stands, wipes his hands together, then looks at me. "That's nice of you, Holly, but I think I can manage walking."

Is he really this stubborn? If he's trying to prove something, I have no idea what it is. Is Port Townsend's big football star so strong and fit that he needs to walk home at three thirty in the morning, even when someone offers to drive him? Give me a break!

As I stand here, looking at him as if he's crazy, Patrick picks up the car jack and tool off the ground and carries it back to my trunk. Shaking my head, I ask, "Where do you live, anyway?"

Patrick walks over to my flat tire and hoists it up to put in my trunk as well. "Across the street," he says casually.

His answer confuses me. "Wait, what? Across the street where?" All that's around here are old buildings full of businesses, so I'm not sure where he's referring to.

Patrick closes my trunk, then walks the few steps over to me. "Right there," he says, pointing behind me.

I turn around and see The Pioneer, one of Port Townsend's oldest hotels. "You live at The Pioneer?" I ask, looking back and squinting at him. Is he joking?

"Yeah, I do," he says. "I bought the place last spring."

My eyebrows nearly hit my hairline. "You did?" To say I'm surprised would be an understatement. How did I not know that Patrick Dye now owns The Pioneer? It seems to me that this would be a well-known fact.

He cracks a smile as he nods his head. "Yep. I started working there shortly after I moved back to town. The owners decided it was time to retire and talked about selling it, so I made them an offer, and they accepted. I live in one of the loft apartments. We used to rent it out to guests, but I figured why not save on rent and just live here?"

"Wow." Patrick Dye is full of surprises tonight.

He reaches out and pats me on the shoulder. "I think you're good to go home now. It's late."

As he starts to walk past me, I turn to look at him. "Thanks again for your help."

He looks back at me. "No problem. I'll see you around, Holly." He winks, and the muscles south of my belly button clench.

I turn around to get in my car. What a night. I'll have to process everything that happened tomorrow, after I get a good night's sleep.

Patrick

Well, that was unexpected.

When I decided to go out tonight, I wasn't sure what to expect, but I definitely didn't think I would end up talking to Holly Seasons. I remember her from high school. Although we were never close, considering she was a year younger than me, she and her sisters were well-known because of their unique names. I always thought she was pretty, and that hasn't changed. Holly is beautiful, and I enjoyed talking with her tonight. I have to admit, while it was unfortunate that she had a flat tire and I don't particularly enjoy changing tires myself, I welcomed the opportunity to spend more time with her.

I can't help but chuckle as I walk into the main entrance of The Pioneer, remembering how shocked Holly was to find out that I own this hotel now. I have to admit that I enjoyed toying with her and getting her riled up when I insisted on walking home. The look on her face when I finally told her I live across the street was priceless.

As I walk through the empty lobby to my apartment, I

think about how relieved I am that I didn't get any calls from guests tonight. I was able to enjoy a night out and ring in the new year without any interruptions. I don't have an employee working the front desk 24/7, but guests can always get ahold of me by phone if they need help with something after hours. I'm usually the one on call since I live at the hotel, but a few nights a week, I pay one of my employees to be on call. I decided to give everyone New Year's Eve off, though.

I unlock the door to my apartment, then go inside. I'm exhausted, so I head straight to bed. It's late, but I was enjoying my time at the bar and didn't want to leave. It's a good thing I stayed, too, since Holly ended up with a flat tire.

I think I'd like to ask Holly out on a date. I wonder when she's scheduled to work at The Cellar again. While I eat there four or five times per week, I rarely see her working when I go. I'll have to switch up my routine and go at a different time in hopes that I'll see her. Of course, it would be easier just to go there and ask one of the other employees when Holly is scheduled to work next. I'll have to do that tomorrow.

After I get some sleep.

* * *

"All I know is that when we went to bed last night, my makeup was in my bag, sitting on the bathroom counter. When I woke up this morning, it was all over the floor." The lady staying in Miss Lucy's room looks at me wide eyed from the other side of the counter.

Her husband stands next to her, looking less than

amused, then speaks up. "Honey, maybe you left it on the edge of the counter and it just fell over in the middle of the night."

She rolls her eyes. "No, that's not what happened. I wouldn't have left it so close to the edge of the counter."

"I'm sorry that happened," I say, hoping this lady won't give us a bad online review. "I hope the rest of your stay here was satisfactory."

The lady half smiles. "Yes, we did enjoy ourselves. Everything was lovely ... until this morning."

"Well, it's a good thing we're checking out then," her husband says. He's clearly not as concerned about the incident as she is.

I'm used to hearing stories like this from guests. Most people don't seem to mind the poltergeist-like experiences, but once in a while, someone will be more concerned and complain--like this lady. If they know about our haunted reputation, though, they're not surprised. In fact, several people stay here specifically because it's known to be haunted. A paranormal TV show even filmed an episode here a few years ago. The Pioneer Hotel is just one of several places in Port Townsend that's had ghostly encounters. This town has a lot of history, and The Pioneer was one of the first hotels to open back in the 1800s. It was also a brothel, and all of the rooms are named after women who worked here.

Having grown up here, I'm a believer. I've experienced quite a few unexplainable things over the years at various locations, especially here at The Pioneer. None of it has ever been evil, though, and I never feel uneasy about it. It's always a little scary in that I'm not expecting something to happen, but it doesn't frighten me. I've come to accept that it's just part of life here.

I finish checking the couple out of their room, then thank them for staying at The Pioneer. Luckily, the wife doesn't seem as upset by the time they leave.

It's almost noon, and I'm ready for a nap. I only got four hours of sleep before I had to wake up for work this morning. I immediately regretted being the nice boss and giving my front desk employees the morning off. I don't know what I was thinking when I thought it was a good idea to work New Year's Eve night *and* New Year's Day. Actually, that's not true. I was thinking that I'd show my employees some appreciation by giving them the time off. I'll have to remember *not* to do this to myself next year.

As much as I'd like to take a nap, though, what I'd *really* like to do is go across the street to The Cellar. I woke up with Holly on my mind, and I'd like to see her again. It's been a long time since I've been interested in a woman like this. I've gone on a few dates since I moved back here, but none of them resulted in a second date. Ever since my last relationship ended, I've been more selective in who I go out with. I don't want to make the same mistake and end up with someone who's superficial.

Luckily, Felicity is due to be here soon, and I'll be off for the rest of the day. My plan is to head across the street for lunch, and hopefully I'll have the chance to talk with Holly again today.

I turn my attention to my computer to do some work. It's not long before I hear the chime on the main entrance and look up to see Felicity walking in. "Hi," she says as she walks toward the counter. "How are things going?"

"Good," I reply as I log off the computer. I tell Felicity all the information she needs to know for the day, then I tell her goodbye and head out the door.

It's a cold, cloudy day, but it's not raining. I briskly walk across the street, then down the stairs to The Cellar's entrance. Walking in the door, I scan the room to see if Holly is there, and I'm delighted to see her talking to customers sitting in one of the booths. She doesn't notice me, so I look around for a place to sit. It's busy, but I find a small table for two to sit at. Hopefully, I'm sitting in the section she's working to make it easy to talk to her. I don't want to interrupt her from working, especially since it's so busy, but I came here for one reason and one reason only––to talk to Holly again.

I look around and watch as Holly waits on other tables. She must be tired after working so late. I wonder what time she had to be here this morning. I know I could use another cup of coffee to help wake me up. I already had a cup this morning, but I haven't eaten anything yet, so I'm hungry. The Cellar serves brunch, and breakfast sounds better than lunch right now. I take out my phone and scan the QR code on the table to view the menu.

After I decide what I want to order, I look up to see Holly walking my way. Her hair is pulled back in a ponytail, and it swings back and forth as she walks. She still hasn't noticed me yet, but I know she will soon. As she gets closer, she's still looking down at the notepad in her hand, but just as she gets to my table, she looks up, doing a double take.

"Oh," she says, stopping in her tracks. "Hi again." Her lips lift into a smile, and she seems to relax a bit. She's obviously busy waiting on several tables.

"Hi. How are you?" I ask, smiling in return.

She runs a hand over the top of her head, then through her ponytail. "Tired," she says with a little laugh. "Thanks again for your help last night. I don't know what I would've done if you hadn't been there."

"It's no problem. I was glad I could help." And that's the truth. No matter how much I hate changing a tire, I was happy to help her.

"Do you know what you'd like to order?" she asks, cutting right to the chase.

"Yeah. I'll have The Cellar Classic and a cup of coffee."

Holly writes my order on her pad of paper. "How would you like your eggs?" she asks.

"Over easy," I reply, admiring her neatly manicured pink fingernails as she writes down my order.

"Would you like bacon or sausage?"

"Bacon," I reply.

"And would you like cream and sugar for your coffee?" She takes her eyes off her notepad to look at me, and I can't help but smile.

"Yes, please," I reply as she looks down and starts to write again.

She finishes scribbling on her notepad, then looks at me again. She has beautiful green eyes, and it occurs to me that the color matches her name.

"I'll be right back with your coffee," she says with a smile, then walks away much too soon.

Damn. I was hoping to talk with her more, but she really doesn't have time for that right now. She stops at the table behind me to see if they need anything before heading back toward the kitchen again. I came at a busy time, and I only see one other server working the floor besides Holly. Luckily, I sat in the right section so I'd have the opportunity to talk with her. But unfortunately, she doesn't have the time to talk right now. Maybe it'll die down before I leave.

One thing's for sure, I want to ask her out. As long as I have enough time to do that before I go, I'll be happy.

As long as she says yes.

It doesn't take long for Holly to return with my coffee. As she sets the mug down in front of me, along with cream and sugar, I suddenly feel weird about the fact that she's waiting on me. I know she's doing her job, but my main objective in coming here was to ask her out on a date, not have her serve me. I guess there's no way around that, though. I'm not exactly allowed behind the bar to serve myself.

"Your food should be out soon," she says. "Can I get you anything else?"

"You're swamped right now, aren't you?" I know the answer is yes, and I don't want to keep her from doing her job, but I'm dying to have a conversation with her that's not just about her getting my food.

She nods. "Yeah, it's pretty crazy for a Tuesday. But I guess that's because a lot of people have New Year's Day off. It feels like a weekend."

"Maybe it'll calm down soon," I say. "Are there only two of you working as servers right now?"

"Yep." Something catches her attention and she looks away, putting a finger up to tell the person she'll be there in a minute. I feel like a dick for holding her back. She looks back at me and says, "I've gotta go. I'll be back with your food in a bit."

"Okay," I say as she walks away. Today is a lot different than last night. Last night, everyone here was having fun, including Holly and the other servers. Sure, they were busy--even more busy than they are now--but everyone was in party mode. Now, the party is over. Holly is doing her job as usual without the fun element last night had. I'm just another one of her customers, and I don't like it. I want to see her more relaxed and have more time to talk with her.

God, I hope she agrees to go out with me.

I stir cream and sugar into my coffee, then take a long sip. While I wait for my food, I scroll through social media on my phone, but my mind is really focused on what I should say to Holly when I finally get the chance to ask her out. I also contemplate where I should take her if she agrees to go out with me.

Before I know it, Holly arrives at my table to deliver my food. "Here you go," she says, setting the plate of eggs, bacon, and hashbrowns in front of me. "Is there anything else I can get for you?"

I glance at the delicious looking food on my plate, then back up at her with a smile on my face. "No, I think I'm good. Thank you." I could ask her out right now, but I'm going to wait until right before I leave. If she turns me down, I want a reason to leave.

"Okay. Enjoy your brunch," she says before turning to walk away again.

I enjoy my food, all the while wondering what Holly will say when I ask her. I haven't been this nervous about asking a woman out on a date in a long time. The past few dates I went on were with women I met on a dating app. We had spent time chatting on the app for a while, and then I asked if they wanted to go out. Easy peasy. This, however, is different. Asking someone in person is a little more nerve racking. I'll be able to see her reaction when I ask her, and facial expressions can reveal a lot. If she's not that into me, her face will show it. I'm really hoping that's not the reaction I get.

Holly stays busy helping other customers while I eat. She doesn't come back to my table, and I wonder if it's only because she's busy, or if she's trying to avoid me for some reason. I try to shove those insecurities away. I tend to be more pessimistic than optimistic, especially when it comes to something I want. I want to go out with Holly, so of course I'm doubting whether or not she'll want to go out with me. I've always been like this, but I've gotten worse since everything happened with my injury. The future I had envisioned for years--and was starting to come true--suddenly got ripped away from me. After everything came crashing down, I try not to get my hopes up so much anymore. That way, when things don't go my way, I'm not as disappointed.

After I finish eating, Holly makes her way back to my table. "How was everything?" she asks, resting a hand on her hip.

"It was good," I reply, leaning back in my seat, ready to turn up the charm and shoot my shot. "It was even better that I got to see you again."

Holly cocks an eyebrow. "Is that right?"

I nod. "It was actually the main reason I walked over here to eat. I wanted to see you again."

Holly shifts her feet, then crosses her arms over her chest. Her lips lift a fraction. "Oh, really?" She seems flustered, and I hope that's a good thing.

I decide to cut right to it. "Would you like to go out sometime?"

There's no going back now. I've asked her. And by the way she's blushing, I think I'm going to like her answer.

"Are you asking me out on a date?" she asks.

I nod. "Yeah, I am. In fact, if you're free later tonight, I'd like to take you out for dinner."

Holly shifts on her feet again, then shoves her hands in the back pockets of her jeans. After a beat, she says, "I'm not off until seven. Although, depending on how busy it is, I may have to stay a little later than that. But if that's not too late for you, we can go out. If you don't mind me looking like this." She points at herself and laughs off her comment.

"I think you look great," I tell her, and it's the truth. "Jeans and a PNWU shirt are perfect for what I have in mind."

She sticks her hand on her hip again. "And what do you have in mind?"

"I don't know," I admit with a laugh. "But anywhere we go around here is casual, so it's all good."

She laughs. "I guess that's true. Okay then. Why don't you give me your number and I'll text you when I get off."

My smile widens as she takes her phone out of her pocket. I give her my number and she saves it in her phone, then sends me a text so I have her number as well.

"Well, I guess I'll see you later, Patrick," she says before turning to walk away.

I reach out and touch her hand. "Wait," I say, and she looks down at my hand on hers, then turns back around to face me. "I need to pay for my meal."

Holly bursts into laughter. "Oh, my gosh. I can't believe I

forgot!" She pulls her notepad out of the front pocket of the apron she's wearing, then tears a paper off and hands it to me.

I don't bother looking at the bill and just hand her my card.

She takes it from me. "I'll be right back," she says before turning and walking toward the bar.

There. It's settled. I'm taking Holly Seasons out on a date tonight. Now I just need to figure out exactly where I'm going to take her.

Holly

What a day. After only five hours of sleep, I was back at work, and it was a busy one. Apparently, a lot of people like to go out to eat on New Year's Day. At least I got paid extra for working on a holiday, and the customers were generous with their tips.

Plus, Patrick came in and asked me out. *That* was a complete surprise. When I first saw him sitting at the table alone, I thought I was seeing things. No way was he back for a second day in a row, but it was true. And then when he told me later that the main reason he came in was to see me again, my heart was in my throat.

After Patrick changed my tire for me last night, I couldn't get him out of my head. I didn't expect anything that happened last night to happen, and the fact that Patrick Dye seemed to be flirting with me made me feel good. Back when we were younger, I always thought he was cute, but I never expected anything to happen between us now that we're older.

Not that anything happened between us. Yet. I have high hopes that our date

goes well tonight. I'm strongly attracted to Patrick, and it's like a teenage dream come true to be going out on a date with him tonight. To be honest, I'm nervous as hell. I haven't been on a date in quite a while. In fact, I haven't gone out with anyone since moving back to Port Townsend.

Now that it's a quarter after seven and I'm finally able to leave work, I text Patrick to let him know. He responds immediately, saying he'll meet me right outside. I take my apron off, check my reflection in the bathroom mirror, then put on my jacket, grab my purse, and leave.

When I texted Summer during my break earlier to let her know I was going on a date tonight, she was happy for me. She was also shocked when I said who the date was with. Although she was older than him and graduated before he was a high school football star, she knows who he is. Honestly, I can't imagine any Port Townsend natives *don't* know who Patrick is. He became quite famous, and he also helped put Port Townsend on the map when he was drafted to play for the Rainier Renegades.

I walk out the main entrance of The Cellar, then head up the stairs. The Cellar has its name because it truly is in the cellar of one of many historic buildings in town. As soon as I step on the sidewalk on the street level, I see Patrick crossing the street, walking toward me.

He smiles right away and waves. "Hey!" He looks even more attractive than he did when I saw him earlier today. He changed into a Columbia River University hoodie--his alma mater--and I wonder if he did that on purpose since I'm wearing a shirt from *my* alma mater. My jacket is now covering that up, though.

"Hi," he says as he walks up to me.

"Hi," I say in return, then can't help but tease him. "CRU, huh? Are you trying to ruin this date before it even gets started?"

His face falls, then he shakes his head. "Insulting my school right out of the gate, huh? I know our colleges are rivals, but I didn't think you were hard-core."

I smirk at him. "Nah, I'm not actually. I just had to tease you." I admire how sexy he looks as his mouth turns up in a smile. "So where are we going?"

"Follow me," Patrick says, and we start walking up Water Street.

It's colder than it was earlier today, and I shove my hands in my coat pockets. There's a slight breeze, and while it's been a fairly mild winter so far, I have a feeling colder weather is on its way.

"How was work?" Patrick asks.

"It was fine. It died down a little after you left, but then we got the dinner rush."

"Do you have to work tomorrow?"

"No, actually I don't. I have tomorrow and Thursday off."

Patrick stops and opens the door to a restaurant I've never been to before. "After you," he says, holding the door open for me.

"Thank you," I say as I walk past him into the Irish pub.

We're seated right away, and we both peruse the menu, quietly deciding what we want to eat. I'm starving, so everything looks good, but I settle on ordering the shepherd's pie.

"I haven't been here before," I say, breaking the silence between us.

"Neither have I," Patrick says. "That's why I chose this place. I've heard good things about it. I'm glad you've never tried it either."

"There was an Irish pub my friends and I used to go to in college all the time. It was right next to campus, and they made the best bangers and mash."

Patrick cracks a smile. "Is that what you're ordering? Bangers and mash?"

"No. The pub by PNWU had *the* best I've ever had, so I'm kind of afraid to order it anywhere else. I doubt it'll be as good, and then I'll be disappointed, so I'm going to get the shepherd's pie instead."

"Well, I'm going to get the bangers and mash, so if you want to give it a try, I'll let you have a bite." Something about the way Patrick says that gives me butterflies. Telling me he'll let me *have a bite* unexpectedly turns me on.

Our server arrives then, and we place our orders. After she walks away, Patrick props his elbows on the table, leaning closer to me. "So what did you study at PNWU, anyway?"

"Elementary education." It's funny how things change. I used to answer that question with pride in my voice. Now, I can't help but hear the slight disappointment in my tone.

"Is that right? My sister is a teacher," Patrick says, taking me by surprise. "She teaches first grade at the elementary school."

"I didn't know that," I reply, forgetting that he has an older sister. She was four years older than me, so I never went to school with her. I still knew who she was, though, thanks to small-town living.

"Do you want to find a teaching job? Or sub?" he asks.

I look down at my hands. Since his sister's a teacher, he'll either completely understand what I'm about to say or he won't, and it all depends on what his sister has said to him about her job. I look back up at Patrick and start to explain. "I'm not really sure. I actually had a teaching job last year."

"You did? Where?" he asks, seeming genuinely interested.

"In Seattle. I got hired at the same school I student taught at."

"Why did you decide to move back to Port Townsend?"

I chuckle nervously. Why do I feel anxious about telling Patrick what happened? "I didn't exactly have the best first year teaching," I explain, hoping he doesn't think I'm crazy for giving up on my career so soon. "I decided to quit, then I decided to move back home."

"Oh, wow," he says, sounding sympathetic. "What happened?"

I begin to explain all of the discipline issues I had to deal with in my class last year. Patrick listens intently, and I get the feeling by the way he nods every so often that he's heard similar things from his sister. The nerves I felt before begin to wash away. By the time I finish explaining it all, our server has returned with our drinks.

Patrick and I both take sips of our beers before he says, "It sounds like you had a rough year. I've heard some of the same frustrations from my sister, so you're not alone. I don't blame you for leaving. I don't think I could've handled all of that either."

"Thanks," I say, relieved he understands. Not that I need to justify my decision to quit my job to him, but it makes it easier that he gets it.

"You should meet my sister. If you're interested in giving teaching another try here in Port Townsend, I'm sure she could help you out. She says they're always in need of subs."

"Thanks." It's kind of him to offer his sister's help. I'm not sure I'll take him up on that offer, but it's still nice. I don't want to continue talking about teaching, though, so I change the subject. "So tell me about you. What was your college major?"

Patrick's eyebrows shoot up. "Well, I actually studied hospitality and tourism management. But I didn't graduate with my degree from CRU."

"You didn't?" I had assumed he graduated college before he was drafted by the Renegades.

"No. I was still quite a few credits short when I left CRU, but I didn't think that was a big deal because I signed a multimillion dollar contract to be a professional football player." He chuckles before continuing. "Little did I know that I would need something to fall back on so soon."

"What exactly happened?" I ask him. "I mean, I know you were injured, but I don't know all the details."

"Basically, I fucked up my leg. I tore my ACL and MCL, as well as broke my tibia and suffered a third degree sprained ankle. It was a freak accident. Joe Dickson, a cornerback who plays for Cincinnati, was trying to block me, and we collided. My ankle rolled, and then he landed on my leg doing the rest of the damage."

I cringe at the image playing in my mind. "Ouch. That sounds painful."

He nods. "It was excruciating. The worst pain I've ever felt in my life. But despite how bad it felt, it was nothing compared to the mental anguish I encountered afterward."

His comment takes me by surprise, and I wonder what he means. Luckily, he continues without me having to ask.

"Obviously, the injury ended my career. After having surgery, my leg wasn't the same, and I could no longer play. Not only did that mess with my mental health, but the hits kept coming. My fiancée cheated on me and left me for another football player. Someone I used to consider a friend."

I have to pick my jaw up off the floor. Did he really just say that? Not only is it horrible that he was cheated on ... I just discovered he was once *engaged*.

"Oh my god," I say. My mind races with questions. Who was his fiancée? How long were they engaged for? Is she from Port Townsend? *Do I know who she is*?

"It's okay," he says, unaware of all the questions I currently have flying through my mind. "It turned out to be a blessing in disguise because I realized exactly what kind of person I was engaged to. I dodged a bullet for sure."

"Wow," I say, unsure of what else to say at the moment. Our server arrives with our food, interrupting our conversation. I rack my brain for how to ask him about his fiancée without seeming too intrusive.

We thank our server and she walks away again. Patrick and I both dig into our food, but I can't get the fact that he was *engaged* out of my head.

"This is good," Patrick says, covering his mouth as he chews. "Wanna try it?"

The shepherd's pie is delicious, too, but I'm curious how his food tastes. I finish chewing, then I take him up on his offer, preparing to be disappointed. I offer a bite of mine to Patrick as well, and we exchange forkfuls of food. When I put his fork of bangers and mash in my mouth, I'm pleasantly surprised. "This tastes just like the place in Seattle," I say, wide eyed. "I should've ordered this for myself."

Patrick smiles, seemingly amused by my discovery. "Your shepherd's pie is delicious, too. This place is as good as the reviews said."

I nod. "It is. I'm glad we came here."

As I take another bite of my food, I consider ways to steer our conversation back to the bomb that he just dropped on me a few moments ago.

It turns out I don't have to, though.

"I'm sure you're wondering about what I told you right before our food came," he says with a nervous chuckle.

I glance at him, then take a sip of my beer. "Yeah ... you were engaged?"

He nods, and I'm anxious to hear all about it.

"She was my college sweetheart. We started dating our junior year. Everything was great, and we fell in love. A year later, I left school to play for the Renegades. After that first season, I proposed to her and she said yes. Still, everything seemed great. However, looking back on things now, I can see how materialistic she was. After I started making money, I was always buying her things she wanted. I even bought her a BMW."

"Wow. That's a lot," I reply, surprised and sad that the woman he loved took advantage of him like that.

"Yeah. Hindsight is twenty-twenty, and she was definitely taking advantage of me." He takes a drink of his beer, then continues. "Anyway, fast-forward to my second season with the Renegades and my injury. She changed right away. When I told her I couldn't play anymore, she suddenly became concerned about how I would make a living. I had so many doctors appointments and physical therapy sessions, and she never went to any of them with me. I later found out that she started seeing one of my former teammates."

"No way," I say. "How could someone do that? Not only her, but your teammate?" What a terrible thing to happen to someone. Being betrayed by the one you love, as well as a friend? That's messed up.

Patrick nods. "Yep. He and I were never close, and in his defense, she told him that we had broken up. They're still together, though."

I shake my head. "I can't even imagine how hard that must've been for you."

"It was hard. I was heartbroken. I decided to move back here and figure out what to do with my life. Although I had quite a bit of money in the bank, I lived with my parents for a while, then started working at The Pioneer. I decided to finish my degree in hospitality and tourism management and found an online program that I completed. Then the owners of The Pioneer decided to sell, and I made them an offer they couldn't refuse. And the rest is history."

I'm still reeling from the fact that his fiancée cheated on him with his former teammate, yet I'm stunned that he moved on with his life and seems so grounded now. He played professional football. He made millions. Then he moved back into his parents' house and earned his college degree online while working at a hotel. Now he owns the hotel. I already liked Patrick, but now I like him even more.

I don't want to dwell on the fact that he was once engaged, especially since it seems insignificant to him now. She's not from Port Townsend, and he has obviously moved on. It shouldn't bother me if it no longer bothers him.

As we continue eating our dinner, it occurs to me that, in a way, our lives parallel one another. Neither of our careers turned out the way we thought they would, and our lives turned out completely different from what we expected. Although our pasts are very different--aside from the fact that we grew up in the same town--I feel as if Patrick and I have more in common than I originally thought.

Our conversation is effortless as we tell each other more about our lives, and it turns out Patrick and I are a lot alike. Time seems to fly by, and before we know it, the restaurant is getting ready to close. It's nearly ten o'clock, and we've been here for over two hours.

Patrick pays our bill, and then we leave. We walk together down the street, back toward my car in The Cellar's parking lot a few blocks away.

"I had a great time," Patrick says. "I'd like to go out again."

A smile spreads across my face. "I'd like that."

"Are you busy tomorrow night?" he asks, filling my heart with joy. It feels good to know that he likes me enough to want to go out again so soon.

"No, I'm not. Would you like to go out?" My heart pounds as I hope he says yes.

"Definitely," he says, looking over at me with a smile on his face.

Patrick walks me to my car, and I wonder if our date will end with a kiss. If I have it my way, it will.

"Will you be able to get your tire fixed soon?" he asks, pointing toward the spare he put on for me last night.

"I plan to take it in tomorrow to see if it can be patched."

He nods, then changes the subject. "I had a really great

time tonight." He steps closer to me, and I wonder if he's going to make a move. I wouldn't be opposed to kissing him.

"I did, too. Thanks again for dinner." My cheeks flush as he steps closer, then reaches for my hands. His hands are warm, and I like the way it feels to touch him.

Patrick looks into my eyes as my heart pounds in my chest. "Can I kiss you?" he asks, moving closer to me.

The heat from his body warms me. I nod once, and he doesn't waste any time. His lips are on mine immediately, and I melt into him. Our tongues glide together as we take this kiss nice and slow. His hand cradles my face, and I wrap my arms around him. His body feels strong and secure, and the scent of his musky cologne hits my senses, turning me on even more. There's not a part of Patrick I'm not attracted to.

He pulls his lips back far too soon, but he doesn't step away. "I like you, Holly." His voice is low and raspy.

Opening my eyes, Patrick and I hold each other's gaze. My belly muscles stir, and it's as if there's a magnetic pull between us. "I like you, too," I say, and his lips curl up into a sexy smile.

"So ... tomorrow, then," he says as his thumb lightly strokes my cheek. "What time are you available?"

"I don't work tomorrow, so I'm free." I feel dazed, captivated by his touch.

Patrick chuckles. "Yeah, you mentioned that before," he says before taking a step back and dropping his hands into his jeans pockets. "Are you free all day?"

Snapping out of the apparent spell he has me under, I miss his touch already, and I wish he'd wrap me in his arms and kiss me again. The fact he wants to see me tomorrow helps ease that ache, though. "Yeah, I am. Except for getting my tire looked at," I say with a laugh.

"I have an idea," he says. "You should take care of your tire first, so call or text me after you do. I want to take you on an adventure."

Surprised, I wonder what he has in mind. "An adventure, huh? Where are you going to take me?"

Patrick steps closer to me again, and I yearn for his touch as I look into his hazel eyes. "You'll find out," he says with a smirk before planting his lips on mine once more.

My body sings with pleasure as my wish for Patrick's touch comes true. I could get used to this.

But Patrick pulls back again, far too soon.

"I'll see you tomorrow. Dress casual and wear tennis shoes," he says, then takes me by surprise when he kisses me all too briefly again.

"O-Okay," I stutter, slightly stunned.

Patrick starts walking away, toward The Pioneer but stops to look at me again. "I'm looking forward to tomorrow," he says, then turns to leave.

I watch Patrick walk toward his hotel for a moment before I turn and get in my car. Holy shit, what a night this was. I like Patrick a lot, and it's exhilarating to know he feels the same way about me. I can't wait to find out where he plans to take me tomorrow. I'm sure our second date will be an adventure like he said it would. There are a million possible things we could do. One thing's for sure--I can't wait to kiss Patrick Dye again.

Patrick

I had to walk away. I had an amazing time with Holly tonight, but I had to force myself to leave before I took things too far. It's only our first date, and I want to be respectful, but if I had my way, I wouldn't be walking into my apartment alone right now.

My attraction to Holly is stronger than anything I've felt in a long time. Not only is she gorgeous but she's also smart, funny, and we have a lot in common. Plus, she's sexy as hell, and based on the kiss we shared, the chemistry is there. It felt as though electricity was pulsing between us, and it was hard for me to say goodbye and walk away.

I can't wait to see her tomorrow.

I can't get Holly off my mind as I get ready for bed. After I crawl into bed, I send her a text.

> I enjoyed our date tonight. Please let me know when you make it home safely.

I turn on my TV so I can catch the scores from today's games. It's not like me *not* to watch college football on New

Year's Day, but this year was different. None of my favorite teams were playing, unfortunately. Plus, I was preoccupied with Holly. And, honestly, I don't mind that one bit.

It's not long before I get a text response from Holly.

> I'm home. :) I had a great time tonight, too. Thanks for taking me out! I can't wait to see what you have in store for tomorrow.

I smile at her text. I need to figure out what we're going to do on our second date tomorrow. As long as it's not raining, I'd like to take her to Fort Worden to explore. I haven't been there since I was a kid, and I've heard from several hotel guests that it's an interesting place to visit. I think it would be fun to walk around the old grounds with Holly, take a tour of the lighthouse, and grab some food at one of the nearby taprooms.

I fall asleep thinking about the possibilities tomorrow holds.

* * *

"Thanks again for staying with us." I hand the couple their receipt, and they smile before turning to leave.

It's good to be the boss. I like working in the mornings, then handing the duties over to my employees and taking the rest of the day off. I haven't regretted buying The Pioneer one bit since I bought it. I love running this place, as well as living here. Port Townsend draws in a lot of tourism because of its rich history, and I intend to preserve the historical charm of The Pioneer and use it to my advantage to draw in more business. The fact that people have paranormal experiences here doesn't hurt, either. I've experienced some unexplainable things myself, but I've gotten used to it. Nothing that ever happens is bad, so if there are really ghosts in my hotel, I don't believe it's anything evil.

My phone rings in my pocket, so I dig it out to see who it is. I'm surprised to see my sister's name on the screen. We haven't talked in a while, and I wonder why she's calling me at eleven thirty on a Wednesday morning. Panic sets in, and I hope nothing bad has happened.

"Hey, Kate. What's up?" I say, hoping that I'm not about to hear bad news come out of my sister's mouth.

"Hey, little bro. How are you?" Kate's friendly and light tone calms my nerves a bit.

"I'm good. How are you? Shouldn't you be at work right now?"

She gives a little laugh, then replies, "Yeah, I am at work, actually. It's my lunch break."

This is odd. Why is Kate calling me from work? She doesn't sound like she's about to deliver bad news, but I'm confused. This isn't like her. "So ... you just decided to give me a call because you missed me so much?"

"Yes, actually ... kind of," she says. "I had a dream about you last night, so I thought I'd give you a call when I had the chance."

"Is that right? Another dream, huh?" Kate has been known to have realistic dreams before. Not just realistic in the sense that they seem real but realistic in the sense that they sometimes come true. It doesn't happen often, but it has a few times in her life. She dreamt I would get a football scholarship, and she was right. She also dreamt that I would be drafted before I graduated college––right again. She's had dreams about some of her close friends, too. It's really uncanny.

"Yeah, I did. Are you seeing someone?"

Her words stop me in my tracks. "Um ... kind of," I tell her. "I mean, we've gone on one date together, but we're going out again later today. Why?"

"Hmm," Kate says as if she's contemplating what to say next. I have to admit, I'm nervous to hear what she has to say about this. Considering how her dreams often come true, I'm not sure I want to know. "Okay, well, all I'm going to say is that in my dream, you were very happy with this person."

My eyebrows shoot up, and I wonder what she's *not* telling me. "Uh-huh ... *and*?"

She laughs. "That's it. It wasn't a very long dream. You brought a woman home to meet the family, and you were happy. That's it."

I laugh nervously. "Okay, then. Well, maybe you'll meet her sometime soon. She's considering signing up to be a substitute teacher."

"Oh really? She's a teacher?"

"Yeah. She taught in Seattle last year, but she decided to move back home, and—"

"Wait!" Kate interrupts me. "She's from Port Townsend? Who is she?"

Crap. Why did I have to say that? I should've chosen my words more carefully. I didn't want to get her all excited about me dating someone. Who knows how far things will go with Holly, and I don't want to get my family involved in my dating life prematurely.

"Patrick," Kate says in her best mom voice. "You know

I'll find out eventually. Especially if she starts subbing. Who is it?"

Rubbing my forehead, I figure there's no use in hiding it. She's right. She'll find out eventually. "It's Holly Seasons. She was a year behind me in school."

"One of the Seasons sisters?" Kate says, her voice rising in pitch. "I know her older sister, Summer. She was a year ahead of me. She still lives in town, too."

"Yeah," I say, nervously rubbing the back of my neck. "Holly is living with Summer now."

"They seem like a nice family. Summer was always nice, anyway." I nod in agreement but don't say anything before Kate continues. "Well, that's cool. I'll keep an eye out for Holly as a sub here."

"Cool. Just keep in mind that we're only going out for the second time today. Who knows if things will progress and turn into anything," I say, not wanting my sister to get the wrong idea. No matter how much I like Holly, I don't want to get ahead of myself here.

"Gotcha," Kate says. "Well, I should get going. My class will be back from recess in a couple of minutes. I just wanted to tell you about my dream."

"Okay. Thanks for calling, Sis."

After we end the call, I consider what she said. Was her dream about Holly, or is it just a coincidence? Only time will tell.

Just then, I get a text notification. I look at my phone and instantly smile when I see that it's from Holly.

I just got my tire fixed. What's the plan for today?

Looking at the time, Felicity is due to be here soon. I reply to Holly's text and tell her that I'll pick her up in about a half an hour.

Luckily, time seems to go by quickly.

When I pull up to Holly's house, nerves take over my body. My heart is pounding, my hands are clammy, and I have butterflies in my stomach. I don't know why I'm this nervous. Our date last night went really well, so I don't think anything will go wrong. I think it's because I like her so much--I want things to go just right today.

Holly gave explicit directions for where her front door was so I wouldn't knock on one of the other units' doors by mistake. I walk up the front porch steps, then knock on the door located on the left side. Within seconds, the door opens, and Holly stands there, looking beautiful as ever.

"Hi," she says, walking out onto the porch and closing the door behind her.

"Hi. You ready?"

"Ready as ever," she replies.

I have the urge to kiss her. She's only a few inches away from me, so I could take her hand, pull her closer, and plant my lips on hers.

But I don't.

Instead, we head down the porch stairs and walk to my car, parked on the street in front of the house.

"This is your car?" she asks, sounding surprised.

"Yeah," I reply, reaching for the passenger side door and opening it for Holly.

"This is nice," she says. "I really like it."

"Thanks." I've gotten a lot of comments on my Audi RS5. I love my car, and I'm grateful I was able to buy it with my football salary. It's silver with tinted windows and fully loaded. It's my dream car.

After she gets in, I shut her door, then round the car to the driver's side and get in.

"So where are you taking me?" Holly asks as I start the car.

"I thought we'd go walk around Fort Worden. I haven't been there since I was a kid, and I've heard it's pretty cool."

"Sounds fun," she says. "I haven't been there since I was a kid, either."

"Field trip in second grade?" I ask.

"Yep." She giggles. "I guess that's the year everyone went."

"Who was your teacher? I had Miss Hall."

Holly's eyes light up. "I did, too! I loved her!"

"She was the best. She's still there, you know. My sister works with her now."

She gasps. "No way! I wonder what other teachers are still there? I really should sign up to sub soon. It'll be a trip to teach at the school I went to."

We continue talking all the way to the fort. One thing I've noticed about Holly is that she's a good listener. She really pays attention to what I say and doesn't always bring the conversation back to her right away, like some people do. She seems to genuinely care about what I have to say, and I genuinely care about what she has to say as well.

When we get to the fort, I drive all the way through to the end, near the battery that overlooks the Strait of Juan de Fuca. It's a cloudy day, but it's not raining. I wonder if it will be clear enough to see Vancouver Island on the other side of the water.

I park the car, and we get out and start walking toward the old concrete battery. We aren't alone; others are also walking around the fort. Even though I want to take Holly's hand in mine, I don't. I want to play it cool and not scare her away by being too forward too soon.

We explore the old battery, which is a bit creepy if I do say so myself. Inside, the narrow halls are dark and echo with any noise that's made. As we walk through one of the hallways, I consider taking the opportunity to kiss Holly in the dark, away from all of the other people here. But the creepiness of the place changes my mind.

"This place is crazy," Holly says as we make our way outside again. "It's like a maze in there."

"Yeah, it is. It's kind of spooky, too," I say with a chuckle. "It's kind of neat to explore, though,"

Holly smiles. "It is. Thanks for bringing me here."

I smile back at her. "Of course. Thanks for coming with me."

We walk to the top of the battery and are greeted with a beautiful view of the water. "Wow," Holly says on a breath. "Even on a cloudy day, it's beautiful here."

I nod in agreement. Looking around, I see that we're alone up here. I don't want to wait any longer--the energy between Holly and me is intense, pulling me to her. Reaching out, I wrap my arms around her waist and look into her beautiful green eyes. I'm relieved when she wraps her arms around me and cracks a smile.

"I've wanted to do this all day," I say as I lower my lips to hers.

We kiss, sweetly, holding one another as we stand on top of this old concrete building overlooking the strait. A breeze blows through, blowing Holly's hair, so I move my hands up and comb my fingers through it. A raindrop hits my forehead, then another. Suddenly, it starts raining on us, causing us to pull apart.

"Oh my gosh!" Holly squeals, pulling her coat hood up over her head.

We head back toward the stairs so we can get back undercover down below. We're not the only ones seeking refuge, though. Several other visitors crowd under the covered areas to get out of the rain, which has turned into a torrential downpour.

"Wow, it's really coming down hard," Holly says as we watch the rain.

I wrap my arm around her shoulder and pull her closer. I look at her, and she

looks at me. "I know I said this last night, but I really like you, Holly."

Her face lights up as her smile widens. "I know I said this last night, too, but I really like you, Patrick." She winks at me, and my cock twitches.

I want her. If I could have it my way, I'd bring Holly back to my place and make her come over and over again.

The rain lets up, turning to a light sprinkle. As much as I'd like to take Holly back to my apartment now, I know it's too soon. Our date has just started, and I have more things planned for us to do.

"Let's go to the lighthouse," I say, lowering my arm and slipping my hand into hers, linking our fingers together.

"Can we go inside?" she asks, her eyes lighting up.

"Yeah, I think so. Let's go see."

We walk to my car, then I drive the short distance across

the park to the lighthouse. We walk hand in hand, and we're both excited to see that we can, in fact, go inside. As we walk in, we admire the old building. We head up the winding staircase to the top of the lighthouse, and when we get to the top, we're greeted by a beautiful view of the surrounding area.

"This is so cool," Holly says as she looks out at the water.

There's one other couple up here with us, but after a short time they head back down the stairs, leaving me alone with Holly. I take this opportunity to get close to her again by wrapping my arm around her waist and burying my face in her neck, kissing her behind her ear. "You smell so good," I tell her. I love the smell of her floral perfume.

She squirms as I kiss her neck. "You smell good yourself," she says with a giggle.

We turn toward each other, and I move my lips from her neck to her mouth, not wasting any time.

"Mmm." A small moan escapes her mouth as her lips part, and our tongues glide together. Kissing Holly is quickly becoming one of my favorite pastimes.

Our kiss becomes more urgent as her hands grip my shoulders. I hold her close, not wanting this kiss to end. But as soon as I hear more people coming up the stairs, I know it will have to.

Reluctantly, I pull my lips away. Looking into her eyes, I decide to be honest with her. "I want you."

She doesn't say anything at first, but her eyes dance with pleasure, and her lips lift a fraction. My arms are still around her, holding her close. Finally, she whispers, "I want you, too."

Taking her hand in mine, I say, "Let's get outta here."

We walk down the winding staircase, then leave, heading

straight for my car. By the time we get in, though, I look at Holly sitting in the passenger seat and realize I don't want to rush things with her. I've rushed things with women before, and where did that get me? Nowhere. Those relationships ended up meaning nothing. I want this relationship to be different. Holly is different, and I don't want to take her for granted. If I take her back to my place now, then what'll we do? I still want to get to know her better first. This is only our second date ... Don't most people wait until the third date to sleep together? I'm not sure I can wait that long, but I know I can at least wait until the end of our date.

"What?" she asks, noticing I'm staring at her, lost in my thoughts.

I quickly shake my head and crack a smile. "Sorry. I was just thinking. I want to take you home, but I also think we should wait a while."

She cocks an eyebrow. "Oh yeah?"

I nod. "Yeah. I want to finish our date as planned first. I enjoy your company, and I don't want to rush things with you."

She smiles, seeming relieved I said that. "Thank you. I appreciate that."

"Good," I say, then start the car. "Are you hungry?"

Holly reaches for her seat belt. "Yeah, I could eat now. Where do you want to go?"

"I know just the place," I say as I pull out of the parking space.

Holly and I go to a nearby taproom to eat a late lunch. We never run out of things to talk about the entire time we're there. One conversation leads to another, which leads to another, and so on. It's just so easy with Holly. My attraction to her is growing, and I can't wait to take her home with me. I only hope she still wants to.

After I pay the bill and head back to my car, Holly asks, "So ... do you have more planned for our date, or are you ready to take me back to your place now?"

Her comment stops me in my tracks. Did she really just say that?

She stops and turns toward me, then laughs. "Sorry ... am I being too forward?" She walks over to me and takes me by surprise again by wrapping her arms around me. "I've had a lot of fun with you today," she says as she looks into my eyes. "But I still want you. Even more than before."

My cock strains against my jeans, and I don't waste any more time. I kiss Holly hard and fast, our tongues lashing against each other. I don't care that we're in a parking lot and other people are around. I don't want to hold back anymore, and I want to get Holly back to my place as soon as fucking possible.

I pull my lips away and rest my forehead against hers. "I want you, too. Will you come back to my apartment with me?"

She nods. "I thought you'd never ask."

We get in my car, then I drive us back toward town.

Holly

It feels like the longest drive ever, but we finally make it back to The Pioneer. Patrick parks in the hotel's parking lot in a spot marked "reserved." We walk hand in hand inside, and he leads the way toward his apartment. I wonder what his place looks like. Is it like a regular apartment, or is it more like a hotel room? As I walk inside, I'm surprised to find that it's a combination of both. It has a living room and kitchen, but the kitchen is small and has smaller appliances than you would normally find in a house or apartment. There's a short hallway with three doors, which I presume go to his bedroom, bathroom, and possibly a closet. It's small but perfect for a single guy like him.

Patrick tosses his wallet and keys into a basket sitting on a table near the door. I set my purse on his couch, then take my coat off.

"I'll take that for you," he offers, so I hand him my jacket, still wet from the rain. He hangs it on a hook near the door next to his. "Do you want something to drink?"

My mouth is dry, probably from nervousness. "I'll have a

glass of water," I say, and he goes to the kitchen to get it for me.

I look around the room, taking it all in. I see a picture frame holding many photos on the wall, so I walk over to look at it closer. I see the photos are all from Patrick's football playing days. Some are from when he played at CRU, and some are from his time with the Renegades.

"Those were good times," he says. I turn around to find him standing behind me, holding two glasses of water. I take one from him and take a sip while he sips his own.

"From what you've told me, it sounds like you had an incredible football career," I say. "I can see how happy you were in those pictures, too."

He nods. "It was a great time. I wish I could do it all over again ... but not get hurt."

"I enjoyed hearing your stories earlier. I wish I knew you back then."

Patrick smiles. God, he's handsome. "Well, I mean, *technically* you knew me ... we just didn't *know* each other."

I laugh. "You got me there." Growing up in a small town where you know everyone yet *don't* know everyone's a little strange. Back in high school, I could never imagine that someday I'd be out on a date with Patrick Dye ... in his apartment, with the intention of sleeping with him.

"I know what you mean, though. I wish we knew each other back then, too." He takes another gulp of his water, then sets the glass on his coffee table and moves closer to me. I take a quick swig of my water, and as I pull it away from my lips, I see the heated passion on Patrick's face. He takes my glass from me and sets it on the table next to his. My heart beats faster as the anticipation builds. The sexual tension has been developing between us, and I want Patrick more than ever. Sure, this is only our second date, but I don't care. We've spent the past three days getting to know each other, and I can't wait any longer.

He takes both my hands in his. "I'm really glad we know each other now."

I nod once, and then his lips cover mine in a scorching kiss. My tongue sensually dances with his as he presses his body to mine. His hard cock presses against my belly, and I'm more than ready to take things to the next level with Patrick.

Patrick's hands glide up my arms, then down my body, sending a tingling sensation throughout. My hands fly to his arms, gripping him like I don't want to let him go. His hands land on my ass, and then he surprises me by lifting me up off the ground. I squeal as he does, wrapping my legs around his waist. We continue kissing as he carries me to his room, not wanting to break apart from each other. But as he lowers me onto his bed, we have no choice but to break our lips apart.

As my back hits the mattress, Patrick begins undoing my pants. I lean up on my elbows to watch him, and he makes quick work of them. I help by pushing the waistband down and shimmying them off as he pulls them down my legs. Patrick drops them on the floor, then looks back at me, a sexy smirk splayed on his lips. I sit up and take my flannel off, then pull my white shirt over my head, leaving me in just my bra and panties.

"Damn, you're sexy," Patrick says, his eyes raking me up and down.

"And you're still fully dressed," I say with a little laugh, hoping he'll strip for me so I can see just how sexy his athletic body is.

He cocks an eyebrow, then stands, pulling his sweatshirt over his head. His taut muscles make my mouth go dry. Patrick has an eight-pack, and I'm dying to run my fingers over his skin. He undoes his jeans, then pulls them off as well. It's my turn to rake him up and down, and the sight of Patrick standing in front of me in only his blue boxer briefs makes my belly flutter. I don't think I've ever been this turned on before.

Patrick licks his lips, then grips the waistband of his boxer briefs, and before I know it, he pulls those off as well. That's when I notice the large scar on his knee, reminding me of his football injury. *Damn.* I can't imagine how painful that must've been for him.

As he stands back up after tossing his underwear to the floor, my eyes move up from his knee to his crotch, and I suck in a breath. His cock is thick and long, and I nearly combust as I watch him wrap a hand around his hard length.

"Do you want this?" he says, his voice husky and low.

I nod. My eyes meet his, and I boldly reply, "Yes. I want you, Patrick."

He moves back onto the bed and straddles my legs, reaching for my silky pink underwear. He doesn't pull them off right away, though. Instead, he runs a finger over my mound. "I can see how wet you are," he says, rubbing my pussy over the silky material. "You're fucking sexy as hell."

He drags my underwear down my legs, then takes them off and drops them on the floor. I need to feel his touch again, to ease the dull ache building between my legs, and luckily I don't have to wait long. Patrick spreads my legs apart, then moves so he's lying between them. My head falls back as his tongue swipes my pussy, taking a long lick all the way up my wet lips.

"Yes," I moan, lying back and relaxing against his mattress as he continues to lick me with his skilled tongue. His hands grip my hips, holding me in place. My body is hot, dying for more, and as soon as he licks my clit, I nearly come apart. Moaning, my hands fly to my bra and pull the cups aside. I toy with my nipples, and the sensations shoot straight down my body. Patrick concentrates his tongue on my clit while he begins to pump a finger in and out. The feeling builds, and before I know it, that tingling sensation explodes, and I call out as my body comes apart.

Patrick moans as well, then sits up and looks down at me. "Fuck, you taste so sweet." He reaches over and opens the drawer to his nightstand. As my body relaxes again and I catch my breath, I watch as he unwraps a condom, then slides it onto his cock. He looks down at me with heated eyes. "You're so sexy touching your tits like that. Take your bra off."

I like the way he tells me to take it off, but I also want *him* to do it. I sit up so our noses are just inches apart. "You take my bra off," I say with a playful smile.

He seems surprised by my boldness but also amused. "Do you like to be dominant in bed?" he asks.

His question catches me off guard. I've never thought about it before. I suppose I do like to be in charge sometimes, but I also like it when the guy takes control. "It depends," I say.

He smirks. "Well, I like to be the dominant one. But ..." He rubs his chin as if he's considering what to say. "The way you just told me to take your bra off turned me on in a way

I've never felt before. I think I like it when you tell me what to do."

Before I can respond, he moves in and kisses me--hard. His hands reach around and unhook my bra, and he takes it off as we continue to kiss. I can taste myself on his mouth, turning me on even more. He lowers me back down onto the bed as we continue to kiss, and then his hand finds my breast. I moan in his mouth, and he moans in return. I'm dying to feel his cock inside me, and luckily, I don't have to wait long.

Spreading my legs, I feel the head of Patrick's cock at my entrance. I'm so wet, he starts to slide in easily. He's bigger than I'm used to, though, so it takes a moment for me to adjust to his size as he slides in deep. I arch my back as his dick hits a spot deep inside that sends tingles through my body. I've never felt that before, and as he slowly pumps in and out, I realize he hits this spot every time, causing me to call out in pleasure.

"You like that?" he asks, moving his lips down my neck.

"Yes ... yes..." My mind goes blank as my entire body builds with pleasure. Patrick picks up his pace a bit, and I know it won't be long before I come again.

He kisses my neck, sucking and kissing all the way down to my breasts. He sucks a nipple in his mouth, and I buck against him as my body explodes again.

"Patrick!" I call out his name as I come undone. He doesn't let up, though. He continues pounding in and out at a delicious pace, and before I know it, I come again. "Fuck, yes!"

Patrick moves his lips to my other breast, driving me insane as he licks and sucks my nipple. My body responds to everything he's doing to me, and I know I'm on the verge of another orgasm. When he pulls his lips away and fucks me harder, I know he's close, too.

"Your pussy feels so good," he says between thrusts.

"You feel so good," I say, my voice barely above a whisper. I'm out of breath.

"I'm gonna come," he says on a breath, and his words do something to me.

"Come in my pussy," I tell him, and he does, calling out my name and setting off

another orgasm for me as well.

"Holly! Fuck!"

As we both catch our breaths and try to relax, Patrick looks into my eyes and

smiles. I smile back at him, realizing this was probably the best sex I've ever had.

"That was good," he says, almost as if he could read my mind. "That was *really* good."

"Yeah, it was," I say, and his smile widens before he leans down and kisses me sweetly on the lips.

"I'd like to do that again," he says, looking into my eyes before he pulls out of me and gets off the bed. "Not now, of course." He chuckles as he disposes of the condom. "But definitely later."

"I'd like that," I say.

We both gather our clothes and get dressed. As I put my flannel back on, Patrick walks over to me, putting his hands on my arms and leaning in to kiss me. It's brief, but I feel as if it holds so much meaning. "I really like you, Holly. I mean that."

"I like you, too," I say as I wrap my arms around him.

"Stay with me. I like spending time with you, and it's still early. We can get dinner later if you want. Let's just hang out and spend more time together."

"That sounds like a great idea," I say, then lean in to kiss him again.

I don't think I'll ever get enough kisses from this man.

Patrick

Valentine's Day

It's been over a month since Holly and I started seeing each other, and I haven't been this happy in a long time. Sure, I was happy with my life prior to meeting her, but once we started dating, it felt as if she filled a void I didn't even realize I had. She makes me feel good, and I love the way her positivity rubs off on me. We just seem to get each other in a way no one else ever did. I don't have to change anything about myself when I'm with her, and I love that.

I'm in love with Holly.

I just haven't told her yet.

Today is the most romantic day of the year, and I have plans for us tonight. I can't wait to pull it all off, then say those three little words to Holly. I'm not even nervous like I had been in the past when it came time to saying *I love you* to a girl. Back then, when I said those words, I wasn't quite sure how the girl would respond. I felt as though I was in love, but

I wasn't sure about them. With Holly, though, I'm fairly certain she feels the same way about me. Our relationship is solid--I know she loves me, too.

Holly has the day off at The Cellar, but she's subbing at the elementary school. She signed up to sub shortly after we started dating, and she stays pretty busy working there. She hasn't quit her job at The Cellar yet, but she did cut her hours back a bit. The nice thing about subbing is that she can turn down a job if she feels she needs a break.

She's also gotten to know my sister through working at the school, and the moment she met Holly, Kate thought we made a great couple. In fact, I took Holly home to meet my parents last week as well, and they agree with Kate. Everyone likes Holly, and it's good to know my family approves of her. In past relationships, that wasn't always the case. They didn't automatically warm up to my ex-fiancée, which I can understand now. She wasn't right for me.

Since Holly met my parents, she's taking me home to meet hers this coming weekend. I'm looking forward to it. All her sisters will be home, too, so I'll get to meet her entire family. It's a little intimidating, but I'm not worried about it. Again, everything with Holly just seems *right.*

I have some things to do to get ready for tonight's date. Instead of taking Holly out, I'm going to cook for her. My mom taught me a few tricks of the trade over the years, and I'm a pretty good cook, if I do say so myself. I'm going to make one of Holly's favorite meals--shrimp fettuccine--along with garlic bread and a salad. I have a few hours to prepare for it before she gets here. She's going to her apartment after work to change and freshen up, then she'll come over. That gives me time to go to the store for all the groceries I need, as well as get a Valentine's gift for Holly.

After Felicity arrives to take over the front desk duties, I go shopping for my romantic night with Holly.

* * *

"Hey, babe," Holly says as she walks in my front door. I left the door unlocked for her, as usual.

"Hi," I say, stirring the alfredo sauce I'm cooking on the stove. "You look beautiful." And she does. As she walks over to me, I think about how lucky I am to be able to call this gorgeous woman mine.

"What are you cooking?" she asks, peering over my shoulder. "I had no idea you were going to cook dinner! I could've brought something."

I shake my head. "No, no, this is my Valentine's gift for you. Well, part of it, anyway."

Holly plants a kiss on my cheek. "This is so sweet of you! I can't believe you went to all this trouble."

"I enjoy cooking. This is my mom's alfredo recipe."

"Wait--you mean you *made* this sauce? It's not from a jar?"

Chuckling, I reply, "That's right. My mom taught me how to make it years ago. I think you'll like it."

Holly places her hands on my face, pulling it closer to her for a quick kiss. "Thank you, babe. This is seriously the sweetest thing anyone's ever done for me!"

"You're welcome," I say, and I have to admit I'm a bit relieved that she's so excited about me cooking dinner for her. It feels good to make her feel so good.

"Can I help with anything?" she asks.

"Nope. You can just take this glass of wine..." I hand her the glass of syrah I had poured for her already. "And go sit down and relax. You've had a long day at work."

She takes the glass of wine from me, her smile widening. "I could get used to this." She winks, then does as I suggest and sits on the couch to drink her wine.

As I finish cooking dinner, we talk about her day of subbing. She worked in a first grade classroom next door to Kate, so she and Kate spent much of the day together. It fills me with joy to hear her talk about my sister as if they're great friends, which I guess they are becoming. It's nice to know that she and Kate get along so well. It's definitely unlike any other relationship I've ever had.

Once dinner is ready, we fill our plates, then sit down at my small table to eat. I light the two long candles I placed in the middle of the table, then dim the lights to give us more of a romantic ambience.

"This is all so amazing," Holly says. "Thank you for doing this."

"You're welcome," I reply with a smile.

Holly takes a bite of her food, and her eyes light up. She moans in pleasure, and

as I watch her with amusement, she points at her food, then gives a thumbs-up. After she finishes chewing and swallows, she says, "This is delicious! Probably the best alfredo sauce I've ever had!"

"That's sweet of you to say. Thank you." I knew she'd like it, but it's a relief to know she likes it so much.

We continue eating while talking about various things. As we talk, I contemplate when a good time to tell her I love her might be. I need to wait for the right moment to make it memorable. By the time we're both finished eating, I pour each of us more wine.

"This was so nice, Patrick," she says as I fill her glass. "Thanks again for cooking dinner for me."

"It was my pleasure," I reply, then take a deep breath to steady my nerves before continuing. "I wanted to make our first Valentine's Day together special."

She tilts her head and smiles. "That's so sweet of you. And it *is* special. I appreciate you being so thoughtful."

I shift in my seat and take a sip of my wine. As I set the glass on the table, I decide to dive right in. "Holly, this past month and a half with you has been incredible. I'm glad that we connected on New Year's Eve, and I've enjoyed getting to know you. We seem to be perfect for each other--we have a lot in common, but we're also opposites in some ways, which I think helps complement one another, too. You're like the peanut butter to my jelly, and not only that, I love how well you get along with my family."

Holly's smile widens. I reach across the table and take her hand in mine, then take another deep breath, hoping what I'm about to say doesn't scare her away.

"Holly, I'm in love with you."

Holly looks at me, her mouth open a fraction, but doesn't say anything. I can't tell what she's thinking, and inwardly I panic. Did I misread her feelings? Did I say this too soon?

Fuck.

Suddenly, Holly's free hand flies to her mouth as she sucks in an audible breath. "Oh my gosh," she whispers. Her hand squeezes mine, and her other hand slowly comes back down to the table. "You love me?"

I nod, wishing I could read her mind right now. Is she happy I said it? Is she freaking out? I still can't tell by her reaction. "Yes, I do. I'm in love with you, Holly."

She just looks at me for a moment before her face breaks into a smile. "I love you, too, Patrick."

Relief washes over me, and I need to hold more than just her hand. I stand, and she stands, too. Our lips come crashing together as our arms wrap around each other. I want Holly. I need her. After bearing my soul, telling her I'm in love with her, I have an overwhelming urge to be closer to her.

Holly moans as her hands claw at my back, and I get the sense that she feels the same way I do. Not wanting to waste any time, I lift her off the floor and carry her to my bedroom, setting her down next to my bed. Immediately, Holly takes me by surprise by dropping to her knees. Her hands fly to the zipper of my jeans, and before I know it, my pants and boxer briefs are around my ankles. She looks up at me as she grips my hard cock in her hand before wrapping her luscious lips around it, taking me in deep.

"Yes," I hiss as my head falls back. She sucks as she pulls her mouth back, then pushes me back in again. I hold the sides of her head, guiding her as she slides her hot mouth back and forth. It feels incredible, and as she continues sucking me, the more it drives me wild.

Then, suddenly, she pulls her mouth off, and she begins stroking me with her hand. "I want you," she says, looking up at me.

Nothing is sexier than seeing Holly on her knees in front

of me, my cock in her hand as she looks up at me through her long lashes. I can't resist her.

"Stand up and take off your clothes," I tell her, and she complies. Holly slowly pulls her shirt over her head, then shimmies out of her pants, leaving her wearing nothing but a sexy black bra and matching panties. "God, you're beautiful," I say, looking her up and down.

She steps toward me and places her hand on my cheek. "I love you," she says before kissing me.

My hands glide up her arms, then around to her back. I unclasp her bra, then slide it off and drop it on the floor before cupping both breasts in my hands, massaging them and pinching her nipples.

Holly's lips pull back from mine, and her head falls back in pleasure. I lower my head to her breast and suck a nipple into my mouth. "God, yes," she whispers. "Don't stop."

I continue pleasuring her nipples with my mouth as my hand dips into her panties. I slide my finger along her wet pussy before landing on her clit, rubbing in circles to work her up. She begins moving her hips against my hand, and she grips my hair between her fingers.

"Patrick," she says my name on a breath, and I can tell she's getting close to her release. She begins stroking me again, and the sensation shoots through my body, making me want her more.

But I want her to come first.

I increase the pressure on her clit, and before long, she calls out in ecstasy. "I'm coming!"

"Yes, baby." I move my lips back up to her mouth and kiss her as she rides out her orgasm.

As her body relaxes, I pull her underwear down her legs,

and then we both get on the bed. As I crawl over her, I stop and look into her eyes for a moment, admiring her beauty. We've said those three little words. We're in love. She feels the same way I feel about her, and it feels amazing.

Her eyes dance with anticipation, and her lips curl up in a mischievous smile. "What are you thinking?" she asks.

I lower my lips to hers and kiss her once before saying, "I"—then kiss her again—"love"—and again--"you." Then I crash my lips to hers in what turns into a passionate kiss.

I line my cock up with her pussy and push inside. Her back bows off the bed, and I pepper kisses down her neck to her breast again. I pump in and out of her, and as she counters my movements, we move at a steady pace together. Holly feels incredible, and sex with her is always good. Better than good, actually. A few weeks ago, we stopped using condoms after discussing how she's on the pill, and both of us are clean. Ever since then, I've felt even closer to Holly whenever we have sex.

"Don't stop," she mews as I flick her nipple back and forth with my tongue. I push in deeper, and she moans in pleasure.

"You feel so good," I say, then bite her nipple gently, causing her to moan again. "I want you to come all over my cock."

I keep fucking her until I decide to roll us over. Holly squeals as I surprise her with the sudden movement, but she doesn't miss a beat as she sits up and starts sliding up and down on my cock. As I watch her ride me, her hands start feeling her own breasts. She's beyond sexy, and she turns me on with every little thing she does. I love watching her ride me, touching herself ... I have so much love for this woman, and I'm suddenly overwhelmed with my feelings for her. How did I get so lucky?

It doesn't take long for Holly to come again. Her muscles clench, and she soaks my cock, setting my own orgasm off. "Holly--fuck!" I call out as my body comes undone.

As we both relax and come back to reality, Holly leans over me, smiling down as she looks into my eyes. "I love you," she says.

"I love you, too." I kiss her, and I know this is right. Holly is right for me. Our relationship is right. For the first time in a long time, all feels right in my world.

Holly

As Patrick drives across town to my parents' house, the windshield wipers struggle to keep up with the rain pounding on the glass. It's a gloomy day in the Pacific Northwest, but it doesn't deter me from my good mood. Patrick holds my left hand in his right, stroking the top of my hand with his thumb, and I feel happier and more content than I've felt in a very long time.

Ever since Patrick and I confessed we love each other, our relationship has become stronger. We're good together. His family accepts me, and I've even become friends with his sister. Now, he's going to meet my family--my *entire* family--and I can't wait for them all to know each other. All my sisters are in town for a few days, so it's the perfect time to introduce him to everyone.

"Are you nervous?" I ask, turning to look at his handsome profile.

He glances at me with a smile on his face before turning his attention back to the road. "I know I should be, but I'm not," he says with a chuckle. "Is that weird?"

I shake my head. "No, not really. I wasn't exactly nervous when I met your family either."

"You weren't?" he asks, glancing at me again.

"No, not really. At least not as nervous as I've been when meeting past boyfriends' parents before. It just felt easy meeting them." I scrunch my nose, hoping he understands what I mean. "Does that make sense?"

"Yeah, it does. I feel the same." He gently squeezes my hand three times, and I squeeze his back three times in response. It's our silent way of saying "I love you."

"Turn right on the next street," I instruct him.

Patrick turns onto the familiar street I grew up on. My parents have lived here for about thirty years, more than my entire life.

"The house is the white one with all the cars in the driveway," I say, pointing to it on the left. "You can park on the street in front."

Patrick drives past the house, then uses the neighbor's driveway to turn around so he can park on the street facing the correct direction. He cuts the engine, then turns to look at me. "We're here," he says before kissing me briefly on the lips.

We get out of his car and walk up to the house. Before we even get to the door, it swings open and April steps outside with a smile plastered across her face. "You're here!" she exclaims with her arms outstretched for a hug.

Patrick and I walk up to her, then I wrap her in a hug. "Hey, April." As we pull away from each other, I introduce her to Patrick.

"It's so nice to finally meet you," April says as they shake hands. "Holly's told me so many nice things!"

"It's nice to meet you, too," he says.

Suddenly, my oldest sister, Autumn appears in the doorway. "Holly!" She bounces out the door and over to me, wrapping her arms around me. "It's been so long!"

We move from side to side as we hug. "I know! Way too long," I reply before we break apart. "This is Patrick," I say, introducing the two of them as well.

Patrick puts his hand out to shake, but Autumn scoffs. "Give me a hug," she says, putting her arms around him. "I don't do handshakes." She laughs as they embrace.

"It's nice to meet you," Patrick says to her. They pull apart from each other, and then we all make our way inside.

As soon as we walk into the living room, Mom, Dad, and Summer are there to greet us. I introduce Patrick to the three of them, and then everyone--all seven of us--sit around the room on the couch, loveseat, and chairs. Everyone asks Patrick questions about himself, and he answers them effortlessly. It's interesting since they're already somewhat familiar with who he is. They just didn't actually *know* him yet.

The conversation flows easily between Patrick and my family. There are lots of smiles and laughter, and he fits right in with us. It makes me happy to see my parents and sisters interacting with the man I love.

After a while, Summer stands and takes my hand. "Time for some sister time in the kitchen," she says, pulling me off the couch as April and Autumn both stand as well.

I look back at Patrick and shrug as Summer pulls me away. "I guess I'll be back," I say to him as we walk away, and he gives me a little wave.

I can't believe he's alone with my parents now. What are

they going to talk about? Hopefully, everything continues to go well.

Once my sisters and I are in the kitchen, Autumn goes straight to the wine rack and selects a bottle. "Here we go! Is rose good, everyone?"

We all agree, and Autumn goes about opening the bottle.

"Okay, girlfriend. Patrick is awesome. Good job." April gives her approval and pats me on the back as we all stand around the kitchen island.

"He really is," Summer says. "I met him once before, and I knew right away that he was perfect for Holly." Summer and Patrick met a couple of weeks ago one day when he picked me up for a date.

"You did good, Holly," Autumn says as she pours the wine into four glasses. "Have you met his family yet?"

"Yes, I did, and they were all great. His parents are very nice, and I really like his sister, Kate. She's a teacher at the elementary school, so I work with her sometimes when I sub there."

"That's awesome," April says. "It's too bad he doesn't have any brothers. I need a man like him in my life." She laughs, then takes a glass of wine and raises it in a toast. We all take a glass and raise ours as well. "To love, happiness, and family!"

"Cheers to that," Autumn says, and we all clank our glasses together.

After I take a sip, I ask Autumn, "How are things going with Cole?"

She blushes. "Things are good. He actually started talking about the possibility of getting married."

My eyebrows shoot up in surprise. “Really? It’s about time!”

Autumn laughs. “Right? I know, we’ve been together forever, but with his family’s past, he’s just very apprehensive about marriage.”

Autumn and Cole have been together for six years now. We’re all aware of his fear of getting married, and I’ve always worried that Autumn is sacrificing what she’s always wanted in life, which is to get married and have a family. To be honest, I’m not exactly sure why she’s stayed committed to Cole for so long when he doesn’t seem to want the same things as her. She insists they’re madly in love, though, and since they live all the way down in Portland, Oregon, I haven’t had the opportunity to get to know Cole very well. I just have to take Autumn’s word and trust that she’s truly happy.

“What’s new in your life, Summer?” April asks. “Any new guys you’re dating?”

Summer shakes her head. “Sadly, no. There aren’t a lot of good, single guys here in Port Townsend. I think Holly got the last available one.”

“Oh, Summer,” I say, rubbing her arm. “You will find the one.”

She shrugs. “I’m good, though. I don’t need a man in my life right now. Seriously.” She takes another sip of her wine.

“I hear that,” April agrees. “But I’m also considering applying for a dating reality show.”

“What?” Summer, Autumn, and I all gasp, and I nearly drop my wine glass.

Did April really just say that? I can’t tell if she’s being serious or not.

She nods and shrugs. "I mean, why not? It works for some people. I might as well put my hat in the ring and see what happens. Chances are, I won't even get chosen. *Thousands* of people apply for each one of those shows."

I guess she's being serious, and, honestly, I can't argue with her. "That's true," I say with a shrug. Her explanation makes sense, and I'll support her if she decides to go through with it. "You might as well try. What's the worst that can happen?"

"Thank you," April says, tapping her glass against mine.

"I don't know," Autumn says with a nervous laugh. "I've watched a few of those shows, and there are *a lot* of worsts that can happen."

Summer nudges Autumn with her shoulder. "Oh, don't be so pessimistic. Maybe April will get chosen for a show and find *the one*."

Autumn shrugs. "I guess you never know. I'll support you if you make it onto a show."

The four of us continue talking for a while before Mom, Dad, and Patrick walk in and join us.

"This is where the party's at," Dad says. He opens the fridge and takes a beer out, then looks at Patrick. "Would you like a beer? Wine? Soda?" Dad asks him.

Patrick stands behind me, placing his hands on my shoulders. "I'll have a beer," he tells my dad. He squeezes my shoulders three times, then I place my right hand over his and squeeze it three times in return before Patrick has to move his hand to take the beer Dad hands him.

As Patrick and I spend time with my family, everything seems natural. I can't believe how well he fits in, yet at the same time, I *can* believe it. Everything with Patrick has been incredible so far. It warms my heart to watch the love of my life get along so well with the people who mean the most to me. It feels as if a new chapter in my life has started––my life with Patrick. I can't see into the future, but I have a strong feeling this is just the beginning of a beautiful, long lasting relationship. Only time will tell what this season of life holds for us.

Read more about Holly and her sisters in C.L. Collier's Seasons of Love Series!

Summer Love

READ THE FIRST CHAPTER OF SUMMER'S STORY, SUMMER LOVE - A SUMMERS IN SEASIDE AND SEASONS OF LOVE CROSSOVER (SEASONS OF LOVE BOOK 2)

Welcome to Seaside.

I roll the car windows down and let the wind whip my hair as I drive into the city limits of Seaside, Oregon. It's been a long day of driving—a little over four hours—and I'm ready to start my week of vacay at the beach with my best girlfriends from college. We get together every summer for a fun, relaxing girls weekend, and this year, we've chosen the small coastal town as our destination.

I slow to a stop, surprised by the long line of traffic. I suppose I shouldn't be surprised, though, considering the Seaside Festival brings a high volume of tourists to the town this time of year. After all, that's the sole reason we've chosen to come. There are several fun activities to partake in while the festival is going on, but what has *really* drawn us here is the Seaside Festival's book signing event, which is featuring several of our favorite authors. Not only are my friends and I avid readers, we're also all librarians. Books are our lives.

"*Traffic ahead. You're still on the quickest route,*" my navigation alerts me.

"Gee, thanks. I couldn't tell," I say sarcastically.

I look at the map and see that I'll arrive at the Sandy Shore Inn in seven minutes. Not too bad. I'm excited to get there, considering I'm the last of my friends to arrive. They've already checked into our rooms at the B&B, and they're currently sitting outside on the deck, enjoying the view with a bottle of wine. I know because they called to see how far out I was about ten minutes ago.

The friends I'm meeting all live in the Greater Seattle area. Michelle drove down from Woodinville and picked Penny up in Federal Way, then they stopped to get Angela in Olympia on their way. Since I'm the only one who lives all the way over on the Olympic Peninsula and took a completely different route to get to Seaside than they did, I drove alone. The four of us met when we attended school at Pacific Northwest University, or PNWU. We graduated seven years ago and have made it a point to get together at least once a year ever since. We used to get together more regularly, but it's become more difficult since they all got married. Penny has a one-year-old daughter now, and Angela's expecting her first baby in December. I'm the only single one in the bunch.

After inching along through traffic, I finally make it to the other side of town and arrive at the Sandy Shore Inn exactly when my navigation predicted I would. The bed and breakfast looks just as it's pictured online. An old Victorian home with a stately turret and wrap-around porch, which according to the online photos, overlooks the beach in the back, about a football field's length away from the Pacific Ocean. I've been looking forward to coming here ever since Michelle suggested this was the place we should stay.

I park next to Michelle's white Camry, then send a text to our group chat to let my friends know I've arrived. Angela replies just as I open the trunk to retrieve my suitcase, telling me that they're still sitting on the back porch, but she'll come inside to meet me. I throw my phone into my purse, get my suitcase, close the trunk, and lock my car, then head toward the entrance of the inn.

The smell of jasmine and patchouli fills the air as I walk in the house. It's lovely. So far, I love everything about this place. The foyer is grand, with a check-in desk front and center. No one is working there at the moment, but that's okay since I don't need to check in. My friends have already done that, and Angela and I are sharing a room. I look to my right and see a gift shop, which looks to be filled with all sorts of New Age things. I'll have to check it out later.

"Summer!" I turn to see Angela walking into the foyer from somewhere in the back of the house.

"Hey!" We walk toward each other and hug. "It's so good to see you!"

"Same! I'm so glad you're here," she says as we pull apart from each other.

"Me, too. This place looks amazing. And you—" I put my arms toward her belly, which isn't showing much yet since she's only a few months along— "look amazing! How are you feeling?"

"So much better," Angela replies with relief. "Morning sickness was horrible throughout the first trimester, but I haven't had it since starting the second."

"That's good," I say, knowing how hard she had it for a while. She has texted us regularly to let us know how she's feeling, and she had felt sick nearly every day for a while.

"Let me show you our room!" Angela points to the staircase leading upstairs. "We're in the Mermaid Room."

"Ooh!" I pick up my suitcase and follow her up the stairs. When I had looked at the website, I saw that all of the guest rooms here are themed. The Mermaid Room is one of my favorites.

Angela leads me to our room and unlocks the door. "Welcome to our abode," she says, opening the door and outstretching her arm to let me enter first.

I walk into the room decked out in seaside and mermaid decor. It's not cheesy or child-like at all. The colors are muted blues, purples, and grays, and it feels cozy and magical. There's only one bed, which we expected, but it's a large king-size, giving Angela and me plenty of space to sleep. We've been friends for so long, this won't be the first time we've shared a bed.

"This looks amazing," I say, setting my suitcase down and taking it all in.

Angela shuts the door behind her. "Michelle and Penny are in the Celestial Room. You'll have to see it later. They have a view of the ocean."

I look out our window, which faces the front of the house. "Lucky bitches," I say with a laugh, and Angela laughs, too.

"Speaking of those lucky bitches, let's go back downstairs and meet them on the porch," Angela suggests. "They have a bottle of wine that I'm sure you'll love."

We head back downstairs, and I follow Angela out to the back deck.

"Summer!" Both Michelle and Penny raise their wine glasses to greet me as we join them. They stand, and I give each of them a hug before we all settle down on the Adirondack chairs situated in a horseshoe shape so we can all see the beach and each other.

"How was your drive?" Penny asks as she pours me a glass of wine.

"It was good, just long," I reply with a laugh. "This place seems amazing, though. Definitely worth the drive."

Penny stands to hand me the glass of white wine, then sits again. "I love it so far, too. I'm glad Michelle found this place online."

I take a sip of my wine. It's a delicious, sweet Riesling.

"So am I," Michelle says. "I was disappointed when the hotels were all sold out, but this place showed up in my search and still had two rooms available. We may have to share beds, but I knew we'd all be okay with that."

"It's totally fine," Angela says before taking a quick sip from her water bottle. "I'm glad they still had availability. I guess this Seaside Festival draws a lot of tourists every year."

"I'm excited for the book signing tomorrow," Penny says.

"Me, too," I reply. "Some of my favorite authors will be there, and I can't wait to have them sign my books."

"Girl, I brought a ton of books with me. I also brought a small cart to haul them around in," Michelle tells us. "I have a list of authors I want to meet!"

"Same," I say, taking another sip of wine.

"Me, too," Penny says.

"Me, three," Angela pipes in, and we all laugh.

We enjoy the sunshine, as well as each other's company, as the ocean breeze tickles our senses. We enjoy the bottle of wine, too, and the three of us polish off a second before we decide to head into town for dinner. Angela drives us in my car, being our designated driver for the weekend.

It feels good being with my friends again. Sure, I have friends back home in Port Townsend—some I've known my whole life, and a few I've met since moving back after college—but my relationship with Michelle, Penny, and Angela is different. We spent our formative young adult lives together and faced several hardships, helping each other through each one we endured. We also share a lot of fun memories. These girls are my rock, like my second group of sisters. This weekend is just what my soul needs.

Read the rest of Summer's story available now on Amazon!

Also by C.L. Collier

Seasons of Love Series

Summer Love (A Summers in Seaside and Seasons of Love Crossover)

Autumn

April

The Salvation Society

Harbor (Shawna's story!)

Summers in Seaside Series

Summer Magic

Summer Love (A Summers in Seaside and Seasons of Love Crossover)

Hot Vegas Nights Series

Playing Vegas

What I Never Knew Series

What I Never Knew

What I Never Knew I Wanted

What I Never Knew I Needed

Discovering Us Series

Stacking the Deck

Finding Our Rhythm

Worthy of Love

Meant to Be

The Vagabond Series

Passion in Paris

Belize Bliss

Visit C.L. Collier's web site

Other books coming soon from C.L. Collier:

Stud Finder: A Limited Edition Romance Anthology - coming February 6, 2024

About the Author

C.L. Collier is a USA Today Bestselling Author who lives in the beautiful Pacific Northwest. She was raised in the Seattle area, and although she lives closer to Portland, Oregon now, she frequently visits the hometown she loves. When she's not writing, you can find her reading, watching her favorite sports teams, spending time with her family, or going to concerts. She likes her music loud, wine and coffee sweet, and her books steamy.

You can find her books here on her website: https://clcolliercom.wordpress.com/books/

Acknowledgments

As I mentioned at the beginning of this book, *Holly* was previously included in *XOXO*, a multi-author limited edition anthology, which was available from February 1 – April 30, 2023. I'd like to give a shout-out to the anthology's coordinator, Ashley Zakrzewski, who is always fabulous to work with. I've worked with Ashley on other anthologies as well, including *Let's Get Naughty,* which hit the *USA Today Best Seller's List* in November, 2022! Ashley always makes the process easy and stress-free for authors to participate in her anthologies, and I want to acknowledge her and thank her for all the hard work she does putting these multi-author anthologies together!

I'd also like to acknowledge Corinne Michaels and The Salvation Society. I was honored to be accepted into The Salvation Society, which is a multi-author series full of books based on Corinne's popular Salvation Series. The book I wrote for The Salvation Society is *Harbor,* and that story's setting and main character led to my ideas for *Holly.* Shawna is the main character in *Harbor,* and it takes place in one of my favorite towns––Port Townsend, Washington. I knew I wanted to write more stories based in PT, and it seemed like the best choice for *Holly* and the Seasons sisters. It also made sense to connect *Holly* with *Harbor* by having Holly start working for Shawna at The Cellar. I love it when books have connections like this!

Finally, I'd like to acknowledge the person I dedicated this book to--my younger sister, Nina. *Holly* is the first book in the Seasons of Love Series, which is a series all about the Seasons sisters. Without Nina in my life, I wouldn't know what it's like, first-hand, to have a sister... and I'm so grateful to have her! Among all the wonderful things she's done for me over the years, without her, I wouldn't have my amazing author logo. Nina is an incredible artist, and I love that I can say that my logo was created and hand-drawn by my own sister! I don't think there are many authors out there who can say that. 😉

Thanks for reading *Holly!* Although Holly & Patrick's story is short, you will read more about their relationship in the other Seasons of Love books!

www.ingramcontent.com/pod-product-compliance
Lightning Source LLC
LaVergne TN
LVHW090533110826
845146LV00003B/1076

* 9 7 9 8 9 8 6 1 4 6 8 3 6 *